George Bradburn, Frances H. Bradburn

A memorial of George Bradburn

George Bradburn, Frances H. Bradburn

A memorial of George Bradburn

ISBN/EAN: 9783743333437

Manufactured in Europe, USA, Canada, Australia, Japa

Cover: Foto ©Raphael Reischuk / pixelio.de

Manufactured and distributed by brebook publishing software
(www.brebook.com)

George Bradburn, Frances H. Bradburn

A memorial of George Bradburn

A

MEMORIAL

OF

GEORGE BRADBURN.

BY HIS WIFE.

———

BOSTON:
CUPPLES, UPHAM AND COMPANY,
Old Corner Bookstore.
1883.

Printed by
ADDISON C. GETCHELL,
4 Pearl Street.

DEDICATION.

O heart of love! O soul of fire!
To thee, beyond, in regions higher,
I dedicate my gathered sheaves,
And pray that I, within these leaves,
May not unfitly store and bind
This harvest of thy heart and mind. —
Thy words of wisdom, wit and mirth,
The loving tributes to thy worth,
Thy brave life-work of voice and pen,
For all thy suffering fellow-men.

CONTENTS.

INTRODUCTION.

To the few remaining contemporaries of my husband, who honored him for his devotion to the great cause so dear to them and to him, and who loved him for his warm and true heart, I hope this Memorial of their friend may have some value. My first thought was to publish it for private presentation only, thus preserving in an enduring form reminiscences precious to his family and near friends. But so many of these friends have urged me to give it a wider circulation, that I have yielded to their wishes, trusting that the absence of literary pretension will disarm criticism.

FRANCES H. BRADBURN.

MELROSE, June 3, 1883.

MEMORIAL OF GEORGE BRADBURN.

CHAPTER I.

GEORGE BRADBURN was born in Attleboro', Mass., March 4, 1806. His father, James Bradburn, was one of the earliest manufacturers of woollen cloth in New England. From his father he inherited his indomitable energy, individuality, wit and fine personal presence.

From his mother — Sarah Leach Hovey — were transmitted to him the conscientiousness which was one of his leading characteristics, the strong religious element permeating his whole nature, and the sensibility which filled his heart with gratitude for all kindnesses of deed or word, and made him so affectionate and loyal a friend. For this mother, who died when he was but eight years of age, he had an idolatrous affection, making her memory the guiding star of his life. Only a few months before his death, in speaking of his hope of meeting her in the next life, he added, "Oh, I fear she will think I have not come up to her standard of goodness; that I shall stand rebuked before her!"

Throughout life, he mourned that he so early lost her companionship and counsel.

This loss was, as far as possible, supplied by the love and care of his half-sister Fanny, Mrs. Waldo Fisher, of Lowell, Mass., for whom his attachment and tenderness from childhood to the end of his life surpassed that of most brothers for own sisters.

For her children his affection was very strong, and the love was mutual. One of them, the Rev. Frederick S. Fisher, performed the last sad office of love for him. His sister survives him, having attained fourscore years; also a brother, of the same union, James S. Bradburn, of Auburn, New York, who has many qualities in common with his brother, particularly the inherited wit which makes his society so interesting to all who know him. There was but one child, besides himself, by his father's later marriage, — Charles Bradburn, for many years before his death an influential merchant of Cleveland, Ohio, and at one time mayor of that beautiful city. He took great interest in the cause of education. The Board of Education placed on the walls of its high school a life-sized portrait of him in oil, taken by special request for this purpose.

George Bradburn was educated a practical machinist, and had a natural talent for the employment. At the early age of nineteen he stood at the head of a large number of employés, most of them older than himself, and many of them twice his age, inspiring and commanding their respect and love by his thorough knowledge of his business, his dignity of manner, and his warm sympathy with their common brotherhood.

If he had remained in this vocation he would

doubtless have accumulated a large fortune, as many of those engaged in the making of machinery did at that time. But his love of study, and desire of usefulness to his race, impelled him to leave it at great pecuniary sacrifice. He entered as a pupil at Exeter Academy; and when he left, having a strong bias for theological study, became a student of the Rev. Mr. King, father of Thomas Starr King, who was very dear to Mr. Bradburn from his earliest childhood.

Soon after, he entered the Divinity School at Cambridge, while there embracing the Unitarian views of Professor Ware, receiving at the termination of his studies there from the American Unitarian Association a certificate to preach.

His first settlement over a church was in Nantucket. While there, he married Lydia Barnard, the only daughter of Capt. Valentine Hussey, a woman of rare personal attractions, beloved by all who knew her. She was of Quaker birth, educated at the Friends' College in Providence, Rhode Island. Her death, in one year after their marriage, and that of their infant daughter in the following year, cast the shadow of sorrow over his whole life. The "dear island," as he invariably termed Nantucket, was inexpressibly dear to him while living there, and ever after cherished by him with tender memories of the noble and gifted men and women who honored him with their confidence and friendship.

CHAPTER II.

IN 1839, Mr. Bradburn was elected to the Legislature by the Whigs of Nantucket.

EXTRACTS FROM HIS JOURNAL.

JANUARY 2, 1839.

Assemblage of the Legislature.

Gov. Everett made his appearance at 11 A.M., and qualified us.

Robert C. Winthrop, apparently quite young for the position, was chosen Speaker.

Dr. Hopkins delivered the election sermon. Text, "Obey God, rather than man."

I am not sorry I was elected to the House. I see not how I could otherwise have done so much for humanity. Though elected as a Whig, yet I cared almost nothing at all for Whiggism, in comparison of liberty, of anti-slavery, of measures and principles technically neither Whig nor Democratic. I have acted, and meant to act, not as a partisan.

Frequently I have found myself voting with the opposition. In Whig caucuses I have opposed projects proposed on mere party grounds. In one of these, the question of voting for the amendments to the Constitution was considered as a question of mere party expediency.

The resolves "on the deliverance of citizens liable to be sold as slaves," which I introduced to the

House, March 6, I have had the highest pleasure in seeing adopted, and signed by Gov. Everett. I accompanied their introduction with a somewhat elaborate report, signed by myself alone, being the only member of the committee in favor of this most righteous measure, all the others having united in a report made by the Senate chairman, declaring it to be inexpedient for the Legislature to take any further action on the subject. When this majority report was agreed on, I was asked by the chairman if I wished to make any report myself. I replied, "Yes, of course I do. I'll take the matter before the three hundred, and if they have heads and hearts, they'll gladly grant all which this committee, whose conduct shall there be thoroughly exposed, has seen fit to deny." The glorious result proved that my confidence in the great body of the Legislature was nowise misplaced. The mass of its members needed but the facts in the case. The committee's truckling subserviency to a corrupt and blind popular opinion, and the legal cobwebs with which those quibbling lawyers had attempted to fetter me, found no favor in the masses of the House when once I had succeeded in getting before them the facts. The debate I entered into with more feeling than I remember to have done into any other. My indignation and disgust at the quibbling, heartless course of the committee, I expressed so freely, and with so much warmth, that Brimmer, of Boston, interrupting me, whispered in my ear that I should lose everything if I were not more moderate. But the villanies perpetrated under those Southern laws are so atrocious, and disconnected as the whole subject is with technical abolition, I felt sure the better and bigger part of the House could be made to sympathize with my own feelings. My expectation was more than met. The House gave me a larger vote than I had hoped for. So did the Senate, where even the chairman of the committee, if he did not vote for the resolves, at least abstained, in deference I fancy to the popular opinion of the House, from opposing them. Dickerson, in the House, was my chief opponent. I think he finally regretted his course, both in the committee and the House. The triumphant passage of the resolves must have surprised him almost as much as one would be by a clap of thunder in a cloudless sky.

The press of both political parties in the city were equally contemptuous with the committee in its treatment of this whole matter. The resolves touching slavery in the District of Columbia, the slave trade, &c., could not be passed with the word "immediate."

The marriage law was the most odious of all the unpopular measures that enlisted my support in the House. The modification of it that was sought, the public would identify with amalgamation. . My constituents, in the outset, were almost universally vexed that I should have meddled with such a matter. The most democratic of the people were the most violent in their prejudices and their opposition. The *élite* of the Boston aristocracy were easier converted than "the hard-handed yeomanry " of the country. A corporal fears familiarity with the rank and file. Napoleon had no such fears. Robert C. Winthrop carried the bill in 1840 by his vote. He made it a point to vote whenever the question came up, departing thus from the Speaker's usual practice of voting only in case of a tie.

George T. Davis, Esq., of Greenfield, who was always a reliable coadjutor in all my measures, whether indirectly or directly anti-slavery, wrote the report against the marriage law in 1840, which from its blind chirography, though I had spent several hours over it, I found so much difficulty in reading to the House that I abandoned the larger part of it to Speaker Winthrop, who possessed a sort of miraculous facility of deciphering such penmanship. My report of 1841 is, I believe, more extended and takes some new views.

George T. Curtis, Esq., about as able a man as the House had while I was in it, spoke repeatedly against the bill, both in 1840 and in 1841. But he was an honorable opponent. During my three years' service in the House, very little was said in favor of repealing this odious marriage law, excepting what was said by myself. In the session of 1839, not another solitary voice was raised for its repeal, and mine was met by a storm of invective and ridicule. Resolved that no time, to say the least, should be saved by the trick of a knot of lawyers and other pro-slavery fellows, in attempting, through the previous question, to prevent me from saying what I wished on the marriage bill, I had taken some four or five opportunities, in debating other questions, to go somewhat into the matter, and to rebuke those who had so meanly trampled on the right of free speech. I had also devised various modes of introducing the question anew. A question once disposed of is not, by the rules, allowed to be re-introduced. I fixed on the following expedient: Petitions are called for at every morning session, by sections. I had taken pains to preserve one (which I think I had got up for the purpose) on the marriage law. When, this morning, my section of the House was called, I sent a batch of petitions to the Speaker in which was the one just mentioned. In this I had purposely omitted to write the reference I would have made of it, taking care to keep my eye on the Speaker as he announced his petitions, with their respective motions of reference to the House. On coming to the one in question, having read its substance, and added as usual, "and moves its reference," he became quite puzzled, as looking on its back he found no motion of reference written there; and casting his eye on me, inquired, "What reference of this petition does the gentleman from Nantucket move?" Rising, I responded, "To the next Legislature. And now, Mr. Speaker, having the floor, I will state to the House some of my reasons for that reference. A certain gentleman of the law, and others in this House, who have made such efforts to prevent all freedom of speech on this troublesome subject, shall now find that those efforts, so far as I am concerned, have been all quite in vain; shall find that at least one member of this House, though all unacquainted with the quibbling clap-trap arts so extensively practised by certain lawyers, is not always with quite absolute certainty to be robbed of his right of speech here, though some pettifogging member may have sprung the previous question on him. I am going to make a speech. [I here pulled a package of notes, documents, &c., from my pocket with all possible deliberateness.] It shall be of such length as I please, and gentlemen not choosing to sit it out have my fullest consent to go out. You, Mr. Speaker, at least I hope to retain. And if I fail to convince the House of the correctness of my views on the subject I am to discuss, I trust I shall not fail to satisfy some, of the impolicy of attempting to save the Commonwealth's time, by gagging 'the gentleman from Nantucket.'" I never knew the House to be taken more by surprise. But all were so patient, and the majority so good-natured, I relented of my purpose, so far as to sit down after speaking between one and two hours.

In the session of 1842, this law was repealed, and people in Massachusetts, wishing to marry, are under no necessity of comparing complexions.

The Board of Education at one time seemed likely to "go by the board." The Democratic influence was against it. Many teachers were against it. Sunday-school book-makers were against it. The Whigs, who had created it, were on the verge of abandoning it for mere party convenience. Several of these were its chief active enemies in the Legislature, as Dodge of Hamilton, and Emerson of Boston. Considerable hostility was felt towards the board's accomplished secretary, Horace Mann, whose Unitarian heresy made him unpalatable to all narrow-souled Evangelical Christians. Emerson is the author

of an arithmetic, and I had small doubts that
his opposition to the secretary, and his operations
against the board, were owing mainly to Mr. Mann's
moderate estimate of that arithmetic. Gov. Morton,
in his message, talked nowise favorably to the board,
though making, I believe, no very direct assault on
it, but talked of the importance of leaving to the
towns — those " little democracies " I think he called
them — the control of educational matters. I believed
the board to be an instrument of great good, though
chiefly so as the means of sustaining Horace Mann,
whom I regarded as doing the State more service
than nine tenths of all its other public functionaries.
I therefore entered with zeal into the support of the
board, which, with its gifted secretary, I lost no
opportunity while in the House of defending against
all attacks, with such ability as I could bring to the
work ; a service for which I have received the thanks
of many estimable persons of influence, both within
and out of the State.

The elective franchise was often a subject of discussion in the House under some form or other. I
did what I could to make it universal, but had almost
nobody to aid me in my own party, and few even in
the Democratic party were disposed to go as far as
myself. I once raised a committee to consider the
subject ; but its members went against even reducing
the poll-tax, which I would have abolished altogether.

The address of the Whigs of the Legislature, in
notice of Gov. Morton's inaugural message, had a
passage on some remarks of the Governor, which I

very much regretted, and which came near from preventing me from signing that address. I refer to its notice of Gov. Morton's remarks in favor of a broader suffrage.

Capital punishment is a barbarism which I labored strenuously to remove from our State, and had the satisfaction at least of seeing the number of offences made capital by our statutes diminished. It was remarkable that the most strenuous opponents of mitigating our bloody criminal code were among the most high-toned professors of religion.

The militia system of the Commonwealth I did what I could to break down as another of its barbarisms. It finally came so near its end as to leave the "service" of its frivolous show to be "performed" by "volunteers." The various "officers" in the Legislature were very "active" in efforts not only to save the system as it stood, but to give it a higher dignity. Some of the most amusing scenes in the House occurred in debates on the militia. At one time even the Shakers were threatened with military impositions. A deputation of the society at Harvard waited on me to solicit my efforts to save them from this apprehended calamity. I took their case before the Militia Committee, and finally succeeded in having Shakers exempted, which just at that time was considered a triumph by some of us.

It was my policy, however, either to exempt *all* professing to be conscientiously opposed to fighting, or none; deeming it meanly inequitable to exempt a sect, as in the case of the Shakers, and refuse to exempt individuals as non-resistants having the

same principles professed by Quakers. I endeavored
to prevent clergymen from being exempted, on the
ground that they possessed no conscientious scru-
ples against fighting. 'Twas amusing to witness the
horror with which this motion was received by
certain military gentlemen, who fancied 'twould look
too bad to have these "messengers of the gospel of
peace," with their bibles and prayer-books, handling
also swords and muskets! They were told that if
war was an anti-Christian practice, Christian legislators had no right to ask, much less to compel, any
to engage in it. If it were a Christian practice, the
superior sanctity of clergymen fitted them all the
better for its discharge. They should all be made
commanders, and their deacons, standing somewhere
between them and the common people in Christian
attainments, should be appointed corporals at least.
I came very near being elected a major-general by
the Legislature one year! Had the joke succeeded,
I should probably have accepted, and so far as one
portion of the militia was concerned, "kept the
peace" for a space.

Imprisonment for debt had always my heartiest
opposition in the House. The bill proposing to
release from the trustee process the laborer's last
forty days' earnings received my support.

Compensation for property destroyed by mobs
was one of the earliest questions I discussed in the
House. I was slightly anticipated by the member
from New Bedford, who brought up the subject. I
wanted full compensation rendered for all property
destroyed by any mob or mobs, by the town or

county in which the destruction occurred. It was finally settled that three quarters of the value of any property so destroyed should be paid for, by the town I think. Such a law, had it existed then, would have met the case of the burning of the Ursuline convent. I omitted no means at my disposal to secure to the owners of this property compensation for their loss by the State. The infernal hatred of Catholics cherished by so many of the "unco pious," and the penuriousness of others, have prevented all justice in this matter.

The "arguments" urged against making pecuniary compensation for this great outrage were too plainly but mere prejudices and passions.

The fifteen-gallon law, identified in so many minds with the temperance cause, was sacrificed to party. It is wonderful how many grave questions are determined on this principle. Three fourths of the righteous acts voted for by either party would, I doubt not, have been voted against had this been thought necessary to secure or to sustain either's ascendency. I voted against the repeal of the fifteen-gallon act, though expressing a willingness to consent to its modification, and did so because its enemies, all "friends of temperance" if you could believe themselves, insisted on its repeal, before stating what they would give us in its place. I would have put wines on the same footing with ardent spirits. O. A. Brownson told me he meant to petition the Legislature to enact a law that ardent spirits should be neither sold, nor bought, *nor drunk*, in any quantity less than fifteen gallons; saying if it was wrong to sell a less quantity, it was equally so to buy or to drink a smaller quantity. I promised to present such a petition if he would send it to me.

The open-ballot law was a strictly party measure, designed by the Whigs to prevent fraud, but defeating the principal purpose of the ballot secrecy.

Such, with the anti-slavery measures, the resolves against the Southern laws, kidnapping our marines of color, and the amendments of our State Constitution, were the chief objects of my interest and action during my three years' membership of the House.

Some correspondent of the "Mercantile Journal" kept an account of all the speeches made in the House in I think 1840, giving the length of each, and its author's name. I was glad to see that some one spoke oftener and consumed more time than myself, who for frequency of speaking and consumption of time was placed second on the list.

But my situation was so peculiar that had I spoken thrice as often and as long as any other member, it surely would have indicated no special fondness for speechifying. For in regard to several measures there were hundreds to speak against them, and only myself to speak for them.

On the anti-slavery resolves in 1840, I think I spoke one day some six hours. Frequently I attempted to save myself from speaking, by requesting some one of similar views to speak for me, but seldom succeeded.

Of the standing committees I was two years on the one on Charitable Institutions (1839–40), and one year on the Committee on Prisons. The former required, among its services, a visit during the session to the Lunatic Asylum at Worcester, the Ear and Eye Infirmary, and the Institution for the Blind in South Boston, and a visit to the State Prison in Charlestown.

Mr. Bradburn, on leaving the House, thanked it for the patient indulgence with which it had listened to his debates, and said, "If in speaking on any occasion I have seemed to express myself with too much warmth; if in rebuking any who have assailed petitioners or their objects I have followed too literally the apostolic injunction, 'Rebuke them sharply,' I can assure the House I have never done so in unkindness of spirit. I have wounded but to heal. It is my fortune to possess a somewhat ardent temperament, and therefore my wont to speak with some degree of warmth as well as elevation of voice; and if in speaking of what seemed to me wrong, either in principle or conduct, I have sometimes appeared to others to speak in anger, I trust it has seldom amounted to anything more than a slight feeling of what divines call 'holy indignation.' I desire to cherish towards all, those sentiments of kindness and good-will which in the retrospect can alone give me peace in the hour of death."

NOTICES OF A FEW PROMINENT WHIG AND DEMOCRATIC MEMBERS.

As a legislator, and as a man of ability, I should rank Charles Allen, Esq., of Worcester, "A No. 1" among these, and none surpassed him in outspoken frankness and honesty. No other Whig member of any standing spoke out so *thoroughly* on all the anti-slavery questions. I do not mean that he made long speeches on these questions, for he debated them scarce at all.

But we all knew how he stood. When George T. Curtis objected to one of my resolutions on the congressional rule, that it charged that rules adopted by Congress were not binding on its own members, Allen defended this (as it seemed even to myself) somewhat ultra opinion.

He would have the representatives of Massachusetts utterly disregard that rule.

Theophilus Parsons, Esq., was a man of most refined manners and personal accomplishments, a winning debater. He used to amuse me by advice to keep cool. Very good advice I always felt it to be ; but certainly as much needed by himself as by any other person.

He was one day replying to an attack of Tarbell's on a committee I believe of which he was a member. Tarbell had intimated the committee was not honest in some of its doings. Parsons trembled like an aspen-leaf, his lips quivering, as looking at Tarbell he exclaimed, "He who accuses *all* men of corruption, convicts of corruption at least *one* man!" I was surprised on learning afterwards that Parsons had been long a principal member of the Swedenborgian Church in Boston, members of that denomination being usually so very remarkable for their calmness. I have not however, meant to say that Parsons was irritable ; he was not.

George T. Curtis possesses, I think, one of the most logical minds in the House. He expresses himself with force and clearness, as well as with considerable deliberation and great distinctness of articulation. But he is very conservative. He advised me to betake myself to the law; was kind enough to say I could gain admission to the bar by a rather short cut.

I told him, what I had on a certain occasion told the House, that I had always fancied there might be more of the law in my composition than of the gospel.

Joseph T. Buckingham is more of a John Bull than I found in any other member. I liked him, however, better than any other prominent Whig among us; there is so much of real independence, and such an entire freedom from cant about the man.

In his very crabbedness I could see something agreeable. I made something of an onset, for me, against some project of his, once; but he never seemed to like me the less for it.

He welcomed me to the use of the "Boston Courier" whenever I should wish to communicate with the public; which under all the circumstances I thought both liberal and flattering.

Robert C. Winthrop, Esq., was the most of an orator among them all, the most finished and classical. His speeches were always very perfect productions. His elocution was equalled by that of no other member. He is, every way, the most accomplished presiding officer I ever knew. I wrote a defence of his perfect impartiality against some im-

putation attempted to be cast on it by the "Post," at
the close of the session in the year 1840. It was
published in the "Boston Courier," over the signature
of "A member of the House of Representatives."

Gen. Grenville Winthrop was the most scholarly
Democrat I met in the House, and perhaps inferior
to none in strength of intellect, as he certainly was
not in the external qualifications of a gentleman.
He was present during my service but a single session. He made but one speech, which was read by
him from a manuscript. It was on the subject of
"Corporations," with which he was chiefly occupied;
going for the right of a Legislature to abolish any
charter granted by any previous Legislature.

I dined one evening at the General's cottage in
Watertown, in company with his brother, Robert C.
Winthrop, George T. Bigelow, Esq., Samuel H.
Walley, Esq., Elbridge Gerry Austin, Esq., George
Phillips, Esq. (brother of Wendell). The dinner
was quite after the English fashion, sitting down at
six or seven o'clock, and not rising till ten or eleven.

Samuel C. Allen, Jr., who was in the House all
the time I was there, was the leader of his party,
though a plain farmer. He deserved to lead. He
had more "gumption" than all his co-laborers, I
used to think; and in management on a small scale,
the tact of a Talleyrand. No villany was ever hatch-
ing but "old Allen" would find the nest and break
its eggs. In more than one instance I was indebted
to his keen insight of such matters for due warning
of some conspiracy to circumvent plans of my own.
He spoke often, but briefly. And when he had

spoken you could always tell how the Democrats would vote to a man. Allen and myself, though not unfrequently measuring swords, were ever on excellent terms. I loved the man. There is a heart in him. He opposes Whiggism because he believes it the enemy of the masses.

It always gave me pleasure to find myself on the same side of any question with Mr. Allen. This happened to myself oftener than to any other Whig in the House, doubtless.

Of the principal Democratic members of the House, they had none who approached Robert Rantoul, Esq., in power of speech and in legal, literary and political attainments.

EXTRACTS FROM THE PRESS.

[From a correspondent of the " Boston Atlas."]

George Bradburn, of Nantucket, is one of the most remarkable men in the House of Representatives; his seat is on the left, and near the Speaker's chair; he may be noticed, during most of the debates, listening with profound attention to the various remarks of the speakers. In consequence of partial deafness, his countenance while listening has a doubtful expression, which, added to the circumstance of his holding his hand to his ear to intercept the sounds, gives an air of incertitude to his appearance somewhat painful. But when he arises to address the House, "all darkness and doubt flee away." Tall in person, unembarrassed in demeanor, bold in language, distinct in utterance, he stands facing the whole assembly, ready at once to give his earnest and decided support, or opposition, to any question, though it might be difficult beforehand to decide which side he will take. Bound by no party ties, and seeing things through a medium of his own, he pursues an independent and fearless course. On all those questions which are by courtesy called philanthropic, though it is difficult in some instances to say why, he will be found an enthusiast.

He is a thorough Abolitionist, and as such attended last summer the "World's Convention" in London, that solemn farce where the male knights-errant were so jealous of the superior intellects of the female ones as to exclude them from their sittings. He is opposed to all the "pomp and panoply of glorious war," as well as against war in the abstract.

He derides the militia and the militia system, and pronounces the whole machinery "absurd and contemptible." He goes to the death for the repeal of the law prohibiting intermarriage between whites and blacks, and though several times put down because New England feelings revolt at the idea, yet he will probably carry his point eventually by sheer teasing and agitation. On the temperance question he is equally ardent, but has wisely let that subject rest this session.

On other subjects Mr. Bradburn may generally be expected to speak and vote on the liberal side of the question. Had he lived in the days of chivalry, no man would have been more ready to couch a lance in favor of the distressed than he; and now, in this calculating age, his heart will always be found in the right place, though his head may be occasionally wrong.

[From the " Anti-Slavery Standard," by Lydia Maria Child.]

George Bradburn addressed the meeting, carrying out Mr. Phillips' train of reasoning, but not confining himself strictly to any point of order. His remarks, as usual, abounded with anecdotes and witticisms, which kept the House convulsed with laughter. No report can give the least idea of his amusing style of speaking; for half the fun lies in the comical gravity of the tone and manner, and the half-suppressed mirth that mantles all over his fine countenance. A thousand sportive Pucks, ready armed for mischief and keen encounter, seem forever lurking in the glance of his eye, the lines of his lip and the motions of his muscles. One sees at a single look that Jeremiah himself could not have helped being mirthful with him. had they met on a barren heath in a midnight storm. From his abundant store of anecdotes the following was told to illustrate the independence of our Northern representatives in Congress : " While they are down there in Washington," says he, " they are very ready to strike under to the slaveholders ; but when they get home, they begin to talk very big about infringement of Northern rights — especially about election time. They shake hands with everybody, and are very particular to ask how you do, and how your wives do. They talk in the bravest style about the rascalities of the South, and the insolence of Southern members of Congress. But down there in Washington they have other business on hand. Their conduct reminds me of a dispute between a good woman (or bad woman, whichever you please to call her) and her husband. Good or bad, she gained the victory over her worse half, as women are wont to do; and he was fain to retreat under the bed to hide from her fury. Secured by this safe entrenchment, he ventured to continue his argument. 'Be silent, you villain!' said she. 'No!' exclaimed he with becoming indignation, 'while I have the spirit of a *man*, I never will hold my tongue!'"

[From other Exchanges.]

Nantucket Bradburn is among them, not unused to the *patriotic* Hall, — the politician, as well as the philanthropist, too honest and too generous and too unwary for party, — the whaleman Bradburn, the thrower of the harpoon in debate. Woe to the fish that encounters him, — whether shark or grampus, or even cod, — for though he does not hear quick, he sees like lightning, and no fin so insignificant or so swift as to evade his unerring throw. An anti-slavery Ishmaelite, —bred in the intellectual wilderness, — where he became an archer, always for humanity, but not always, or often, on the side of the multitude.

Did you ever, Mr. Editor, hear George Bradburn? He was present at the Convention, and made a short speech. He is an orator *sui generis*. His gestures, intonations and emphasis are all his own. A strong man, he uses almost exclusively the strong old Saxon dialect. As Novalis said of Luther's, "his words are half battles." He has no superfluous language; all his sentences are full of condensed thought. His powers of wit and sarcasm make him a dangerous opponent, as more than one ex-member of the Massachusetts Legislature can testify to from his own sorrowful experience.

The resolutions appended to the report of Mr. Bradburn of Nantucket, touching certain laws of slaveholding States which affect the rights of citizens of Massachusetts, have been adopted by both branches of the Legislature with great unanimity, and with only one or two slight verbal amendments.

This is another triumph of humanity over prejudice and tyranny, which will long and honorably identify the name of Mr. Bradburn with the legislation of Massachusetts.

He has on all occasions acquitted himself with rare ability, true independence, and great moral courage.

The accompanying pen-and-ink sketch of George Bradburn was drawn by Dr. Elder of the "Washington National Era:" —

It represents him as he appeared at the Buffalo Convention in 1847, which "made as much stir as a convention of buffaloes."

"Looking all around the crowd, as if 'hearsay was no evidence' to him that he was called for until he saw the call in the nods and smiles of a hundred friends, and then turning up his *pure, transparent, hydropathic* face and fair cylindrical neck, spreading out his right hand to get all the points of his

subject at his fingers' ends, and swelling his chest to
lay in breath for the whole speech, he dashed away
with mingled mirth and edged earnestness, playful
wit and pointed logic, plump into the delicate questions that everybody else would have said grace over
and asked forgiveness before making the attack.
Assailing open enemies and timid friends, confess-
ing his own sins against the party, and chastising
others that are now in the same condemnation, kick-
ing compromises, tickling the leaguers, poking fun at
their leaders, all in one medley mass, mixed up with
great broad, beautiful benevolence, lofty principle,
single-hearted honesty and profound philosophy,—
all poured out as impetuously as if his vocabulary had
the whooping-cough and uttered in a voice that cut
like a circular saw, to the tune that it caught from the
file which sharpened it.   Altogether the speech made
such an impression on the multitude that they would
take nothing else till they had taken their dinners,
and so the first session adjourned; every one feeling
that anything might be said, at any time, to any-
body, if George Bradburn were the speaker."

CHAPTER III.

IN 1839, Mr. Bradburn was appointed an agent of the American Anti-Slavery Society, giving all his time and support to the cause *in its infancy*, when to be a champion was to be despised and persecuted. And in the days of its power and efficiency, he gave all his talents and eloquence to its advocacy. His last labors in that capacity were in attending the famous "One Hundred Conventions" planned by John A. Collins, in 1843, "a campaign of five months, every inch of which was disputed by mobs, indifference and coldness." Near the close of this tour, he was stricken with a fever at Cincinnati, which left him prostrated for many months.

In July, 1839, he delivered an oration before the Anti-Slavery Society in Boston, of which a few extracts are given, as showing his accurate information on all topics connected with his subject, his ardent enthusiasm, and his great moral courage in thus daring at such an epoch to attack this sin "in all high places."

EXTRACTS FROM ORATION DELIVERED IN BOSTON, JULY 4, 1839.

After accepting, a few days since, the invitation with which I was unexpectedly honored, to address you on this the sixty-third anniversary of our nation's independence, I asked myself what I should say.

Not that I was anxious to utter a new idea. I had
no such anxiety, and if I had, it were probably vain.
But what could I say that would be appropriate to
the occasion? To pursue the course usually adopted
by our fourth-of-July orators I certainly could not
consent. It would be as contrary to my convictions
of duty as unwarranted by facts. For what is their
course? What on this our national birthday is the
chief vocation of our hundreds of young men who
get up into the high places to speak? Why, what
but the playing of a great national game of brag, —
the utterance of indiscriminate eulogium of our
country, our institutions, of ourselves, and of an
equally indiscriminate censure, not always unmixed
with abuse, of the institutions and the people of other
countries?

Such, you know, is the course adopted by the herd
of your fourth-of-July orators. And especially is it
true of them that while they never forget to recount
in glowing words the wrongs and the oppressions
endured for a season, but soon nobly thrown off by
our revolutionary fathers, and to praise most patri-
otically everything American, they are none the less
intent on doing valiant battle against old England,
as if the *present* inhabitants of that country were the
authors of the evils inflicted upon our fathers. But
such (I said to myself in answer to my own question) is not the course I will take. It is not the
course which I have marked out for myself on this
occasion. And if it be the one which any who have
come up hither had expected me to pursue, I can
only say that however much I may regret the disap-

pointment to which I shall subject them, I can have no sympathy with the views and sentiments which must lie at the basis of that disappointment. I came not here to play the part of a mere panegyrist. But although I have little to say in flattery of our national vanity, and still less in gratification or encouragement of our national hates, I yield to no person in sincere love of my country, or in ardent disposition to promote her true honor and glory. Undoubtedly the day on which we have met is calculated to awaken thrilling recollections, and to swell with just pride and with joy the bosom of every American. It is a day of rejoicing. Most fitting is it that we observe it. With good reasons may it ever continue to be so observed. But it ought — for the present at least — also to be observed as a day of sorrowing; for it is not more certainly calculated to awaken in us as a nation, sentiments of joy, than to provoke reflections which should fill us with sorrow and humiliation. We should rejoice with trembling.

Threescore and three years this day, there was put forth to the world, the most extraordinary instrument ever presented to the attention of mankind; an instrument which, while it has excited the astonishment, has won also the admiration, of the friends of freedom and humanity throughout the civilized globe. I allude, of course, to the Declaration of American Independence, whose sentiments and whose history are familiar to almost every child among us, however imperfectly their spirit may be now appreciated and acted upon by the mass of our men and women. But

what is it that has stamped this instrument with a
character of such extraordinariness, and filled the
hearts of all lovers of liberty with so deep and peculiar an admiration of it?   Shall we seek the answer
to this question in the peculiar circumstances which
gave birth to the instrument?   Shall we refer to the
character and situation of its illustrious authors, to
their intense love of freedom and burning hatred of
tyranny, to the oppressions they endured, to the
loftiness of soul, the firmness of purpose and the
calm self-reliance and Christian confidence they exhibited?   All these, it is true, should not be left out
of consideration ; they are, indeed, worthy the pro-
foundest study and reflection, as well as calculated to
inspire high admiration.   But in them alone we find
not that answer, though they might sufficiently account for the fact of the American Revolution.   The
extraordinary character of this instrument, and the
peculiar admiration it has everywhere elicited, are
owing not so much to these or to any similar circumstances as to the doctrines of the instrument itself,
not abstractly considered, but as adopted and proclaimed to the world by the representatives of a
whole people as the foundation of all just governments.   This it is that stamped the Declaration of
American Independence with its character of extraordinariness, and inspired the friends of liberty
throughout the world with so unique an admiration
of it.

And what are those doctrines?   They are, in the
brief yet comprehensive words of the Declaration, as
follows :   " We hold," say the authors of that instru-

ment, "these truths to be self-evident — that all men are created equal; that they are endowed by their Creator with certain inalienable rights; that among these are life, liberty, and the pursuit of happiness; that to secure these rights governments are instituted among men, deriving their just powers from the consent of the governed;" and, "that whenever any government becomes destructive of these ends, it is the right of the people to alter or to abolish it, and to institute a new government." These are the doctrines which, viewed in connection with the design of making them the basis of the government that was yet to be established for the American people, shed over the Declaration its brightest lustre, which impart to it its distinguishing, its peculiar glory, which constitute it the greatest instrument ever yet put forth to the world. And it is these which have won for it such universal approbation from the friends of freedom and humanity.

The announcement of these doctrines to the world by so august a body of men as self-evident truths and as the basis of all just governments, was calculated to make tyrants and oppressors quake with fear. Against autocracies, hierarchies, oligarchies, and whatever other forms of government that were not based on the eternal principles of right and the natural equality of mankind, it was the severest condemnation that could be uttered. It was a declaration of moral war against the whole of them, and consequently against every government then existing upon the face of the earth.

It was not, therefore, to be expected that these

doctrines, self-evidently true though they were, would be regarded with much favor by the interested supporters and abettors of such governments. Of course, when doubted, denied and scorned by them, as they soon came to be, their friends can have experienced no disappointment. It was just what was to be looked for. Neither was it to be expected that these doctrines could be sustained, be made the basis of a government for this nation, as an independent people, with small expense. Nor were they. They cost our fathers much blood and treasure. They subjected them to a seven years' war with the most powerful nation on earth; and this perhaps was not the greatest, if among the greatest, of the expenses incurred in the establishment and practical maintenance of the self-evident truths of the Declaration. But it was to be hoped that none claiming to be Americans would ever be found to carp and cavil and sneer at these self-evident truths so dear to our fathers. But in this the friends of those truths have been disappointed.

Take, for instance, that of the natural equality of men, — all men are created equal. How much carping and cavilling and sneering have we not heard at this proposition, and by those who boast themselves to have descended from the men who pronounced it a self-evident truth !

"All men," say these wiseacres, "are *not* created equal. It is a lie upon the face of the Declaration. Why so? Because we see that some are born to poverty while others are born to wealth; some to a superior, others to an inferior condition of life;

some are created geniuses, others ignoramuses. It is nonsense, therefore, to affirm, as the Declaration does, that all men are created equal." Such is the mode adopted by not a few as well to disprove as to ridicule this self-evident truth. As if the authors of the Declaration were fools enough to affirm that all men are created equal in respect to outward advantages of mental endowments, or of physical size, symmetry and configuration. An equality of *rights*, not of intellectual and moral qualifications, still less of outward condition, was what they meant to assert. Hence these wiseacres, but for their imbecility of mind and perverseness of heart, would do well to read the Declaration again and endeavor to get at its meaning. Of the infamous purpose their sophistry and satire are designed to subserve, it is unnecessary to speak. It is but to gain some sanction for the denial, which is also made by these scorners, of two other self-evident truths of the Declaration; namely, the inalienable right of all men to liberty, and the inalienable right of all men to the pursuit of happiness.

Thirteen years after the adoption of the Declaration of Independence the organization of the government of these United States was completed by the adoption of the Constitution. That Constitution recognizes — it does not sanction, as some imagine, much less does it agree to perpetuate — the "institution" (to use the euphemism by which its friends choose to designate the bloody system) " of domestic slavery," an institution which tramples on all the principles of the Declaration; denies that all men are created equal; denies that all men have the right to liberty and the pursuit of happiness; denies that to *secure* these rights, governments are instituted among men, deriving their *just* powers from the *consent* of the governed. But is there then a conflict between the principles of the Constitution and those of the Declaration? Does not the former embody, and is it not founded upon, the self-evident truths of the latter? Its own preamble states its object to be — among other things — "to establish justice," "promote the general welfare, and secure the blessings of liberty to its authors and their posterity." This was certainly the design of the framers of the Constitution. It was obviously their purpose not only to make the Constitution consistent with the self-evident truths of the Declaration, but to make it also the instrument of carrying those truths into practical operation. But whether the two instruments are perfectly consistent with each other, is a question with some minds. But it is a question which I am not going to discuss. I will only say that I cannot see how the mere recognition of slavery can be construed into a sanction of, or even as an apology for, the system. Were that system to be this day abolished, the Constitution might remain as it is, it would require no alteration to be adapted to the new state of things. But that slavery was felt to be repugnant to the principles of the Declaration by those who formed and adopted the Constitution, there can be no doubt. No honest man ever pretended to doubt it. It was shown to be so — to say nothing of the numerous other proofs of the fact — by the pains taken to avoid all mention of the system by name.

John Randolph, himself a large slaveholder, but who happily was led to repent that crime before going to his final account, once in his place on the floor of Congress said, "I thank God that the Constitution of my country is not stained by the word slavery." It is well known too that at the time of the adoption of the Constitution the expectation was general, both among the supporters and the enemies of slavery, that so terrible an anomaly could not be long tolerated under a professedly free government. And it is believed — not without sufficient reasons either — that but for this general, this confident expectation, the Constitution had never received the sanction of a majority of these States. The debates in the conventions of the different States furnish of themselves strong proof of this fact.

Since the adoption of the Constitution our country has greatly prospered, presenting almost from that moment a striking contrast with its miserable, feeble condition under the articles of confederation. Its prosperity, indeed, has been without a parallel in the history of nations. From a little handful of three millions, we have become a great and a powerful people. In wealth our increase has been in a larger ratio. The number of our States has doubled. Immense regions of territory, a half-century since a dense wilderness, disturbed only by the tread of wild beasts and savages, have been transformed into fruitful fields, smiling villages and thronged cities, the abodes of industry, of civilization and refinement. Internal improvements, commerce and manufactures have flourished, perhaps beyond all former precedent. Education, on which more than anything else the success of all free governments must ever depend, has participated in the general prosperousness of the country. If our standard of education is not so elevated, nor the relative number of our thoroughly educated men so large, as in the fatherland, we may still boast this great advantage, that the blessings of education are here more widely diffused among the people.

For these, and for numerous other circumstances of prosperity enjoyed by our country under the Constitution, we have, as a people, great cause of thankfulness, of joy and gratulation. And this is a most fitting occasion for the free indulgence of these feelings; since it is the anniversary of that great event — the Declaration of American Independence — which led to the establishment of that Constitution which, under God, has proved the chief source of the unprecedented prosperity of the nation.

But, as I have already intimated, we should wrong ourselves, and our country also, were we to make this anniversary an occasion of exclusive festivity and of national self-congratulation. The sun of America is not without its spots, and whoever looks on it and sees none has not the eye of a republican. He has not the vision of a New Englander. As a nation we have, it is true, great reasons for rejoicing. But it is also true that we have equally great, I fear much greater, reasons for sorrowing, for humiliation, for deep contrition. I could not avoid speaking of the former; I will not abstain from alluding to some of the latter.

. . . .

But I must conclude. I have spoken of the reasons which on this occasion should inspire Americans with joy and gratitude, and also of those which ought to excite in us sentiments of sorrow, of humiliation, of deep contrition.

It may be inferred from what has been said, that the latter predominate over the former. On that point I have no opinion to offer. It has been my object to state facts. From these each individual may draw his own inference, form his own opinions, and govern himself accordingly. Let no one, however, infer that I despair of republicanism. *I have faith in man. I believe in human progress.* I cannot, therefore, despair of the triumph of free institutions, of genuine republicanism. But the experiment of free institutions, of republicanism, so far at least as America is concerned, remains to be made. *The American Republic is no Republic. It is an abuse of language, it is solemn mockery, it is sheer nonsense, to call that a Republic in which every sixth man is doomed to slavery!* Hence I have no sympathy with those, numerous as they are, whose only hope of the success of free governments is based on the American experiment. Suppose that experiment should fail, as some believe it will: what then? What would it prove? Anything against the practicability of free institutions? Not at all. It would prove that a government pretending to be free while holding a large portion of its citizens in chains, had failed — was unable to perpetuate itself. And that is all it would prove. The failure of such an experiment could disappoint none but hypocrites and tyrants. It should in no wise diminish the faith of any friend of liberty in the practicability of true republicanism. Should this nation be dashed in pieces and be no more heard of forever, it would furnish not the slightest ground of triumph to the enemies of freedom. It should extinguish not one ray of hope now beaming on the minds of its intelligent friends. If liberty may not be established in America, its establishment elsewhere may be hoped for. But I hope for its establishment here, if not by the men now living, by those of a future and a worthier generation. There are, moreover, grounds of hope to which I have not adverted. I see such grounds in the efforts of those by whose invitation I stand here to address you. Some eight years since and there was but a single voice heard in our land in denunciation of the mountain-crimes of this nation. Now that voice, then so like that of "John the Baptist crying in the wilderness," is echoed and re-echoed by thousands.

Nor do I know that it should be deemed any abatement of these grounds of hope, that slight divisions touching certain extraneous, though not unimportant, questions chance to have sprung up among the enemies of slavery in this part of the battle-field.

The evils of these divisions, I trust, will be more than compensated by the benefits likely to arise from them. They will shed light which is everywhere greatly needed on two great questions; I mean the respect due to conscience, *and the importance, especially in all great moral enterprises, of the aid of women.* Anything that will throw light upon these questions must be productive of good. It must operate beneficially upon the cause of the slave. Socrates was not ashamed to attend lectures given by a woman on philosophy. A Christian apostle was glad to avail himself of her aid in extending and establishing the doctrines of the gospel. The practical results that seem likely to grow out of the present divisions among the friends of the slave, may show that abolitionists, not less than Socrates and Paul, can derive assistance from the labors of women.

I see grounds of hope in the public sentiment of the old world. That sentiment cannot tolerate slavery, and it deepens and spreads daily. And nobly, most nobly, is it uttered by the Broughams, the O'Connells and the Thompsons of our fatherland. There has been lately established in England a society whose object is the extermination of slavery throughout the world. She has also set us a glorious example in the emancipation of the 800,000 slaves of her colonial possessions, an example which is exerting a great and an increasing influence in favor of emancipation on the minds of our own countrymen, who, strange to say, needed an experiment to satisfy them of the safety of obeying God. And a similar experiment, it is said, is to be made by the Pasha of Egypt, who contemplates the speedy emancipation of all the slaves in his dominion. It is hoped that so glorious an exemplification of the spirit of Jesus by this Mahometan will not be wholly lost upon our Christian republic. In these facts I see amid all the gloom and sorrow naturally inspired by the adverse ones which have been referred to, grounds of hope, — I may add, of joy and gratulation. Our principles are evidently spreading, silently it may be, but certainly and even rapidly, both at home and abroad. Mighty movements are going on through the world in favor of the masses. Everywhere there are manifestations of sympathy for the oppressed. The prejudices of caste are disappearing, and wherever the attributes of humanity are found, respect is beginning to be cherished for the man, *as man*. The sympathy which is manifested for the slave, and the efforts that are made in his behalf, are but an outbreaking of that great sentiment of liberty and equality which is beginning to move the nations of the earth. To the progress of this sentiment, men may, as we have seen many now do, set themselves in opposition. But that opposition can avail nothing. The cause of freedom which is the cause of reason, of justice, of God, — the cause in which our revolutionary fathers fought and bled and died, — it must be, will triumph. Such is its destiny. And men may, as well think to chain the winds, to roll back the swelling floods of the Mississippi to their source, or to stay the cataract of Niagara with a straw, as to prevent the ultimate triumph of the principles of universal liberty and equality.

CHAPTER IV.

APPOINTMENT AS DELEGATE TO THE WORLD'S CONVENTION, LONDON, IN 1840.

HOW long and how ardently have I desired to see the land of my fathers! And now I have a prospect of realizing that earnest and long-cherished desire, having been appointed a delegate to the Convention of the Friends of Freedom throughout the World, to be held in London in June. I find the "Roscoe," in which the Philadelphia Abolitionists, with some other delegates, are to sail, does not leave till the 7th of May. I supposed she might sail to-morrow, else I should have remained some days longer at home. The "Roscoe" is a fine ship, and I have secured a good berth.

May 1. — Excursion to Philadelphia. Not seeing how I could better employ the leisure now on my hands, I occupied it in an excursion to the City of Brotherly Love, going thither on the first and returning on the sixth. Met the great Scotch phrenologist, Geo. Combe, at Mrs. Mott's at dinner. Mr. Combe has an exalted opinion of Mrs. Mott, and his favorite science could scarce stand, were she not worthy of it. It was a treat to meet this philosopher, and I regretted to see so little of him, for he left the house after remaining a couple of hours. Mr. Combe favored me with a letter to Dr. Richard Carmichael, of Dublin, and another to Mr. Deville, of

London. Hon. Horace Mann was expected at Mrs. Mott's. We were greatly disappointed that he was not present. I took pains to find him, but without success. I afterwards learned that he endeavored to find me, that we were mutually anxious to see each other. I learned also that he would have been at Mrs. Mott's but for some misunderstanding on the part of Mr. Combe, whom Mrs. Mott had requested to invite him. Mr. Combe doubts if we have a greater among us than Mr. Mann. If Mr. Mann would visit Scotland, England, &c., and labor in behalf of education there as he does here, Mr. Combe would regard the event as the dawning of an era unequalled almost by any other since the advent of our Saviour. That is a tremendous compliment; but of Mr. Mann a phrenologist *must* think highly, whether he looks at his head or at what he has done and is doing. To-day Whittier handed me a copy of his paper ("Pennsylvania Freeman"), containing the following article from the Roman Catholic journal of Boston. I had not seen it before, and am glad I had not. 'Twould have been a " delicate matter " to have corrected, as I might have felt moved to do, the "Pilot's" mistake of my politics. Perhaps though the able editor of that print may have intended to compliment me by using the word "democratic" in its *true* sense. "In the same paper (the Boston "Pilot") we find the following eulogium upon our Abolition friend, George Bradburn: 'Among the Democratic members of the Legislature we particularly observe George Bradburn, of Nantucket, the fearless advocate of human rights, whether popular or unpopular, the unyielding opponent of bigotry and exclusiveness, let them take what shape they will. He unites the frank simplicity of a child with the intelligence of a sage.'"

Returned to New York May 7. At a little before eleven A.M., having with some effort got all things in readiness, I went on board the steamer that was to take the passengers on board the "Roscoe." At a few moments past eleven the steamer put off to the ship which lay in the East River, and taking the "Roscoe" in tow we were soon out of the harbor. We were towed some five miles, when our sails were unfurled to a favoring breeze, the steamer was detached and we stood nobly out to sea. Many of the passengers were attended by friends till the ship and the steamer parted company, when the tears in many an eye told how painful it is for friends to separate. The scenery of the bay of New York is more beautiful than I had supposed. At six and a half o'clock we were out of sight of land. Shall I ever see it again? I watched it as I did the setting sun, till it seemed to sink beneath the wave. May I return to it a better man, and better armed for the duties of a man!

May 8. — Some fifty miles to the southwest of Nantucket. Could I but run in and take a cup of tea with some of my friends! Large numbers of the stormy petrel are following in the wake of our gallant ship. What tireless creatures! One wonders how they can keep so perpetually on the wing.

May 9. — Was surprised on going up on deck at 8 A.M. to find a severe storm. The wind was dead ahead, and it soon increased to a gale. The passengers were all or nearly all sick. Poor Mrs. Mott was very sick. In the afternoon I became so, but continued so only a short time, an hour or two, and might perhaps have avoided all sickness, rough as the sea and weather were, had I dined less freely. We ran all day under a topsail only. In the evening the wind abated.

May 11. — During the day multitudes of porpoises were seen around our ship, disporting themselves at a glorious rate. I had before no conception of the prodigious strength and agility of these fish. They seemed bent on showing us that the "Roscoe's" ten knots an hour speed was scarce a circumstance to theirs, and cleft the water as an arrow does the air, sometimes leaping from wave to wave, or rather shooting through them and exposing their whole forms in the open atmosphere of the intervening hollows. It was a real entertainment to us landsmen.

There are about thirty passengers in the cabin. James Mott and his wife, Misses Abby Kimber, Sarah Pugh, Elizabeth Neall, Rev. Henry Grew and his daughter (Mary), of Philadelphia, Miss Abby Southwick, of Boston, and Isaac Winslow and his daughter (Emily), of Portland, cross the water to attend the convention. We have as agreeable a company of passengers as one could well hope to find in any packet ship. And our captain (Huttleston) is a gentleman every inch of him. My outward man is in excellent condition. I like the sea, at least I like the bounding over it in the "Roscoe," and know not when I have experienced a deeper consciousness of joyous existence. Rev. Mr. Dewey, who declares he felt nothing of seasickness, complained of inability to be pleased with anything in crossing the Atlantic. I am quite disposed to be pleased with everything.

Was called by the captain at 11 P.M. to see a beautiful lunar rainbow, to me an entirely novel sight. Its hues were fainter than those of the solar rainbow, and this was the only peculiarity I observed in its appearance.

May 17. — Experienced another storm more severe than the former one. Indeed, it was tremendous. Our captain said he was never out when it blew harder, and he has crossed the Atlantic a great many times and " weathered many a storm." One of the mizzenmast yards was broken off in the midst as though it were a thing of straw. The rain fell in torrents ; the sea ran little mountains, now and anon dashing its spray furiously over the whole ship, which rolled and pitched frightfully. But it was a scene full of sublimity, one which I would not have missed the observation and experience of for a great deal, though I care not to witness the recurrence of another such.

May 24. — To-day being Sunday, religious services were held in the cabin. The last Sabbath none were attempted, in consequence of the storm. Mr. Grew officiated. The subject of his sermon was the necessity of faith, of faith in the atonement ; a sort of necessity which I apprehend he did not succeed in making clear to all present. He was followed by Mrs. Mott. There was little congruity between the

two sermons.   Mrs. M. urged the importance of love
and of good works as alone sufficient.   But the per-
ception of disagreement or want of harmony between
sentiments uttered by the two preachers may have
had the good effect of setting some of the hearers to
thinking.   There are unthinking hearers, as well as
forgetful hearers of the Word.

May 25. — With the gentlemen from the West
Indies, passengers, I have had on several occasions
some conversation and discussion touching the abolition of slavery in the British islands.   Dr. McNaught,
one of these, deemed it uncharitable to call the slaveholder a man-stealer.   They represent emancipation
to have worked badly for the planters, in Jamaica at
least, but well for the negroes; that the latter will
work only when they please ; that they do not always
please to work when the interests of the owners
require that they should do so; that consequently
there has been a diminution in the value of estates,
and a falling off in the products of the same.   They
designed their remarks should apply especially to
Jamaica.   In the other colonies, which are more
thickly populated, and because more thickly populated, they suppose things work more favorably, that
is to say, to the planters.

They insist that the negroes will not work so
cheaply as they should.   But their greatest difficulty
appears to be that the negroes will work only when
they have a mind to do so ; that, like their employ-
ers, they will work when they choose and play when
they choose.   And the means of subsistence are so
easily available that the negroes may live by laboring

only a very small portion of the time. They say the responsibility of slavery in the British West Indies belonged to England, she by her legislation having forced it upon them. The £20,000,000 granted by Parliament to the planters, they allege, was altogether inadequate as a compensation for " the property" taken from them, and affect great indignation and scorn at its being called a " compensation." It was gratifying to be able to meet all they said in disparagement of the negroes, or of the excellent working of the great experiment, by a great array of facts drawn from documents of governors, magistrates and eminent planters and others of the colonies themselves, and from the reports of parliamentary committees, as well as from the many and very full statements of persons (both Abolitionists and non-Abolitionists) who had visited the islands for the express purpose of examining into the condition of things there. It is a remarkable fact that many of these West Indian croakers omit no opportunity of buying property in the islands. It is an old trick of sharpers to decry the wares they would buy.

May 26. — Entered the St. George's Channel. At dinner we had parting toasts and speeches. I was taken by surprise, yet I inflicted my speech. Messrs. Winslow, Whitwell and myself drank our toasts in cold water. This seemed odd to others, and some thought it was insulting to drink the Queen's health in water.

Reached the magnificent docks of Liverpool at 8 P.M., having been towed up the rapid current of the Mersey by a steam tug. At the invitation and by the advice of Captain Huttleston, our Abolition party remained to-night on board.

Custom-house officers are aboard to see that there is no smuggling. But the protection of the government, I infer from what the captain tells me, comes not of the honesty of those fellows, whose pay is not enough to keep soul and body together. The passengers who went on shore, left their baggage to be taken in the morning to the custom-house, excepting a few articles they were allowed to take as a matter of favor. The prospect from the "Roscoe's" deck this evening was fine. There was the noble Mersey with its unrivalled docks, crowded with forests of ships; and along the line of the river to the extent of some two miles blazed innumerable gaslights whose brilliant rays were reflected by the water. I find my arrival here attended with less joy than I had once anticipated; with less, because I am not so anxious as I supposed I should be to get on *terra firma.* Indeed, I could have quite rejoiced to be on the ocean another fortnight, so greatly have I enjoyed this passage of the Atlantic. High health, a fine ship, favorable weather (saving the two storms), a gentlemanly captain, attentive servants, a faithful crew and a pleasant company, including several valued friends, — how, amid all these comforts, *could* I be specially pleased at the idea of their being broken in upon by our arrival on this side of the water? Could I be sure of getting back so pleasantly to America, what delight I should find in the assurance !

Liverpool, May 28. — At six A.M. we all came on

shore and took lodgings at the Adelphi, which is to
Liverpool what the Tremont is to Boston. The servants
who waited on us at breakfast are such a set of fellows as an American is in some danger of mistaking
for an equal number of the nobility. It was painful
to Mrs. Mott to see them in such a capacity, or
rather to allow herself to be waited on at table by
men capable of services of so much greater consequence.

Liverpool wears a dingy appearance, but its streets
and buildings seem orderly, firm and substantial.
The bricks of which many of the houses are built,
appear to be a third larger than ours. Its public
edifices have little about them worth an American's
notice. Its docks are its greatest, its only wonder;
but these I have not yet particularly examined. I
apprehend Liverpool is not *very* English, in outward
seeming at least.

Before dinner, the Unitarians of our party were
invited to tea at William Rathbone's, the ex-mayor.
Found Mr. R. an agreeable and a very intelligent
man. As a business man, and as a citizen, I should
judge he must stand high; and was not surprised on
making his acquaintance that he should have filled
the office of mayor of the city. The late William
Roscoe was an intimate friend of Mr. R., and, like
him, was a devoted Unitarian. A daughter of Mr. R.
is the wife of one of the Unitarian clergymen of this
place.

We talked of America, of Unitarianism, of Channing, Gannett, Dewey, of the "Liverpool controver-
sy," of the corn laws, church rates, &c. I was not

less pleased with Mrs. R. than with her husband. She is an uncommonly bright woman, and possesses great conversational powers. I was struck with her young appearance, and would have taken her to be the daughter, rather than the wife, of the ex-mayor.

In religious matters, in Unitarianism and its advocates, she evinces a deeper interest than even her husband. I was delighted to hear her eulogize Dr. Priestly. I had expressed an opinion that his merits had never been sufficiently acknowledged by the American Unitarians, which I attributed partly to the unpopularity in our country of that great divine's doctrines of necessity and materialism; observing that of those doctrines Channing himself appeared to entertain a strange horror. Mrs. R. thinks the English Unitarians are still essentially necessarians. She spoke of a meeting of great interest, held some time ago in honor of Priestly's memory.

Speaking of the corn laws, Mr. R. said that public opinion in respect of them varied with British crops. When these were scarce, the corn laws were comparatively forgotten. Hence, said Mr. R., it was wittily remarked by an Irishman or a Frenchman — I forget now which, but most probably the former — "that the English are a nation of ventriloquists."

Mr. Rathbone's residence is about three miles out of the city. We found it a delightful drive, and were charmed with the place also; a beautiful cottage, with green hedges, gardens, trees, and verdant lawns, a sort of "Mahometan paradise."

Rev. James Martineau was expected to be present, but did not come. We called at his house on our way thither. He was not at home. We returned to the Adelphi at about ten o'clock, our whole party being highly gratified with our afternoon and evening's entertainment.

May 29. — I spent an hour or two in rambling about the city in the morning; visiting the Huskisson Cemetery, which contains a statue monument of the celebrated Huskisson, who came to so untimely an end on the Liverpool and Manchester Railway. The Cemetery is a curiosity. It is an immense hollow, formed by the quarrying of sandstone, of several acres in extent, and of an oblong form, its walls rising nearly perpendicular to the height of a hundred feet or more.

Rev. James Martineau called on us at the Adelphi; but as we were about to leave the city, we had the pleasure of his company only a few moments. He complained that their American friends could never be induced to stop any time in Liverpool. But we had the satisfaction of promising ourselves another meeting. In Manchester, he said, we should see their "white slaves." He is a Cassius-looking man, has a dark complexion, and seems like one who works hard. His sister Harriet is at Newcastle-upon-Tyne for the benefit of her feeble health, yet having some work on her hands.

The journey from Liverpool to London may be made by railroad in a day. But we concluded to make it more leisurely, for the purpose of touching at sundry places of interest; not caring should we not reach the metropolis much before the sitting of the convention on the 12th proximo; so we took a coach for Chester.   It was a bright sunny day, and brought to my mind Dr. Johnson's description of the pleasures of an English stage-coach ride, which I never before so fully appreciated.

We reached Chester in time for a late dinner; an Englishman would say an early dinner.   This is one of the old walled towns.   A part of the wall now remaining is said to be Roman.   I foresee that my faith is to be severely tasked.   Those of large marvellousness have at least one enviable quality as visitors of these old places.   The principal objects of interest in Chester are its walls, its castles, its cathedral, its St. John's church, its sheltered sidewalks, and the bridge of stone spanning its fine river by a single arch.   The cathedral was built in the seventh century.   Among its relics is one of the tombs of the first Earl of Chesterfield, nephew of William the Conqueror.   St. John's church was built at a still earlier period.   The apex of one of its gothic arches is clasped by the dividing branches of a considerable tree which has sprung up beneath it, the trunk having divided itself into two nearly equal parts just at the point necessary to save the arch, as though Nature herself had grown reverent of this venerable ruin.

We made an excursion to Eaton Hall, the enchanting palace of the Marquis of Westminster, formerly Lord Grosvenor.   The elaborately cultivated grounds, in the centre of which stands the hall, occupy an area of seven miles.

The entrance is through a fine arched gateway. One approaches very near the hall before seeing it, the sight being intercepted by the boughs of numerous trees. We notice in passing herds of deer and flocks of peacocks and other birds. There is nothing very striking, except perhaps its great length, in the exterior of Eaton Hall, but within it is rich and beautiful beyond, I had almost said, everything I had expected to see in England.

The great hall into which we were first ushered is hung around with shields, helmets, spears, swords, carbines, pistols, suits of armor of various material and workmanship, trophies of the chase, &c., &c., the arrangement of all of which, as of all else we saw here, indicated a liberal endowment in some one or more of the organs of order and ideality.

Exquisite pictures and statues adorn the rooms. We observed among them several of the Marquis and other members of the family. The Marquis must have a most prepossessing person, and a countenance almost rivalling in its expression of benevolence and quietude that of the Apostle John.

The library contains a valuable collection of books, but its numerous mock-volumes are unworthy of such a place as Eaton Hall, though they may serve its owner's purpose as well as real ones. The chapel is in good taste. The hall is four hundred and twenty-five feet long, and is soon to be extended to four hundred and seventy feet. A spacious aisle or avenue runs its whole length, and at either end of the aisle is a magnificent stained window. Sandstone is the material of its walls, which are of great thickness, and its floors for the most part, I believe, are of polished oak. From one end of the hall is seen a sheet of water amid trees and verdure, and from its rear, as one passes into the gardens and at the distance of several miles the land on the right rises to a considerable elevation till at length the view directly in front is partially terminated by a jutting out of the highest portion of it into the plain, like the projection into the sea of some lofty headland. I was never before so impressed with the folly of all attempts of tourists to convey by words an adequate conception of such places as Eaton Hall. It were wisdom itself in comparison with that device of the person we read of, who, to convey an idea of the splendor and value of a palace he wished to sell, exhibited a single brick.

The pen of a Scott might perhaps without presumption undertake such a task, but one of feebler powers of description had better let it alone. Eaton Hall to be known must be seen, as conscience to be known must be felt.

We left Chester soon after an early breakfast this morning, taking, as before, outside seats, and arriving at Manchester about 2 P.M.

I went to the Unitarian chapel here this morning. Was invited to take a seat with a gentleman to whom after the service I was introduced as the mayor of the city, Mr. Potter.' The chapel is a very plain building, somewhat resembling in structure as well as in simplicity an old-fashioned New England meeting-house. If one may judge after the outward appearance, I should say Unitarianism does not flourish in Manchester quite "like a green bay tree." It was a thin meeting on a bright, pleasant day.

There is a new sort of Friends here. They adopt some of the forms of the Episcopal Church.

What a sad falling away from the simplicity of primitive Quakerism!

Here I find there are Bradburns. I wish I had time to ascertain whence they originated. Perhaps the bones of some of my ancestors mingled centuries since with Manchester earth. The birth place of Samuel Bradburn the famous Methodist preacher I cannot remember. It would delight me truly to make the acquaintance of some of my namesakes here. I have sufficient reasons for believing that the greatest noblemen in the three kingdoms are descended from their and my great ancestor, the renowned Lord Adam of Eden.

The Mechanics' Institute contains a grand collection of models of ingenious machines, fabrics, &c., to which our annual exhibition of similar things in Boston is scarce a circumstance. Saw there an electioneering autograph letter of William Cobbett addressed to people of Manchester, and appointing a time to speak to them on matters and things involved in the then approaching election. It was characteristic, and interested me as much as anything I saw. It detailed among other things his labors for some three or four weeks prior to its date; as if to admonish the people of Manchester that he also was a workingman. And William Cobbett *was* a workingman if ever there was one. His labors through a long life were prodigious, and when I think of them I am amazed.

Leaving Manchester yesterday we arrived at Birmingham in the evening. This is literally "a city set on a hill." One would suppose it must be healthier, as it is obviously cleanlier, than Manchester, which stands on nearly a dead level. It is by far the pleasantest business place we have yet visited. The town hall, market, and free grammar school are well worth looking at. An American would be proud of the last edifice as a university building; though the market, saving for its mammoth dimensions, is unworthy of comparison with our Boston market.

Dr. Priestly once resided here. It was here that the great theologist and philosopher had his house pulled down about his ears, and his valuable manuscripts and library destroyed. But mobbing Unitarians did not extirpate their heresy. I suppose there were Unitarians among the "gentlemen of property and standing" who mobbed Garrison, Harriet Martineau and other Abolitionists in Boston. Joseph Sturge resides here, but has gone to London to prepare for the convention.

June 2. — Taking coach at three P.M. we arrived at Warwick between six and seven. It being too late to get admission to the castle, we spent an hour or two at the "Hospital of the Twelve Brethren," and at the Church of St. Mary adjoining it, both very ancient; the latter a mere ruin. The hospital, originally a monastery, was founded by Robert Dudley, Earl of Leicester. It is a most singular charity. It was established for the perpetual support of twelve poor men who should belong to the county in which it is located, and have been in the naval or military service of the crown. If, however, there should be

at any time a deficiency of men in this county to
make out such a number, it was provided that the
deficiency might be supplied from elsewhere. Such
comfortable paupers I had never dreamed of as existing out of the royal family. Each has a suite of
well-furnished rooms, and an annuity of eighty
pounds sterling. Their cooking is done at the expense of the hospital. If married, as several of the
present incumbents are, they have their wives with
them. They look and live and act quite like affluent
gentlemen in retirement. We learned that when
they meet in the public room to "fight their battles
o'er again," disputes sometimes run high among the
brethren, as they do among brethren making professions of greater holiness. They have a neat chapel,
and a chaplain to *do* their religion. We were told
that this building was visited by Queen Elizabeth,
and that James I. was once entertained in it.

June 3. — Warwick Castle is the finest existing
specimen of the old English baronial castle. At the
lodge we were shown Guy, Earl of Warwick's
armor, walking-stick and porridge-pot, which is of
stone and will hold two barrels. The old earl's
armor, including that of his favorite horse, and his
walking-stick, correspond in bulk and weight to the
porridge-pot. Verily, "there were giants in those
days." The castle is an enclosure of perhaps eight
acres, and one would think the walls of this enclosure might defy all the artillery and battering-rams
of old England, they are so huge. Warwick Castle
is not so beautiful as Eaton Hall, but it has an air of
grandeur that gives it a much deeper interest. One

of its massive walls is washed by the river. It has some glorious pictures of Rubens, Titian, Vandyke, and other distinguished artists.

After breakfasting we ordered carriages and made an excursion to Kenilworth. The ruins, which are even more extensive than I had imagined, tell one plainly enough it was once all "the wizard of the north" represents it to have been. But how can I write of Kenilworth and Warwick Castle? How paltry are all the descriptions given of them by tourists when compared with the impressions received from the actual observation of them!

Immediately on returning from Kenilworth, we set off for Stratford-upon-Avon. We looked at the pinched apartment in which the poet was born, recording our names in the visitors' book. Thence we strolled to the old church containing his remains and those of his wife, which are covered by a plain coarse flat stone. Think of standing on the tombstone of Shakspeare! There seems something awful in its inscription. But for it his remains would probably have been transferred to Westminster Abbey, which was not a fit place for the remains of Shakspeare. The room in which he went to school was pointed out to me. Went into the "Garrick Gallery," containing a statue and a picture of him. In the latter there is such an expression of intense thought, glowing with ideality, that one wonders how it could have been transferred to canvas. It represents the poet with a pen in his hand, sitting over his manuscript, the eyes turned slightly upwards, as if moulding one of those wonderful creations of his. I never before left a picture so reluctantly.

We arrived at Woodstock in season to take a view of Blenheim Palace, the nation's splendid gift to the Duke of Marlborough as a reward for his brilliant military services. We rambled through the beautiful walks and over the bright greensward of its magnificent park. Blenheim Palace was once a royal residence, and in richness and grandeur it excels all I have yet seen. The property of our Girard was an insignificant trifle in comparison of this present to that old general; for it must be remembered that in making it, the government provided also for its appropriate maintenance in all coming time. And surely, if England can thus reward her military heroes, who will wonder that men should be ambitious to fight her battles? The park is many miles in circumference, and we noticed large numbers of deer roaming over its velvety carpet of "living green." The rich old oaks on the right of the palace are so arranged as to represent the order in which the Duke's regiments were drawn up in his famous battle. In front of the palace, and at the distance of perhaps a mile and a half, stands a lofty monument surmounted by a colossal statue of the illustrious general. The inscriptions on it are of great length, including the act of Parliament in full, I believe, by which these princely possessions were conveyed to the Duke of Marlborough and his heirs forever.

We reached Oxford on the fourth, and found no difficulty in gaining admission to the colleges, churches and such other places as we desired to see.

To us the Bodleian Library was the greatest wonder of Oxford.

I noticed in the library a picture of Addison on his death-bed, admonishing his wayward son-in-law. The windows of the church of New College are ornamented with full-length pictures of patriarchs, prophets, apostles, &c. We were shown the spot where Ridley and Latimer and Cranmer suffered. It is in the centre of the busiest streets. The college buildings look very old, as most of them are. They are of a soft dull-colored stone, a material miserable enough when compared with New England granite. But its softness is favorable to ornament.

We arrived at this old world-famous Windsor at 5 P.M., and having secured lodgings, we mounted to the castle. It was too late to gain admission into it, so we contented ourselves with strolling through its courts and avenues, and promenading the lofty terrace which overlooks the great park, said to be fourteen miles in circuit. The Round tower commands a view of twelve counties. What enormous piles of sandstone! The edifices are so numerous, and so oddly constructed withal, I find it hard to obtain a conception of even their general outlines. They impress me with emotions rather than with ideas.

Who has not heard of Eton school? Its location is just over the river. This being the anniversary of the birth of George III., it was a joyous time with Eton boys. I went with several of our party to the banks of the Thames to see them return from a row-boat excursion up the river. They came down in gallant style. There were nearly a dozen boats of a long, light, narrow construction, which were managed with a tact and skill worthy of high admiration. Such a fine, healthy, energetic company of pupils I never before saw. The boats passed backwards and forwards for an hour or two, performing numerous admirable nautical evolutions amid a profusion of blazing rockets, serpents and other fireworks. The whole was enlivened by music.

June 5. — Before breakfast we made a visit to the school. It was too early to see much of the scholars. The seats and benches were covered with marks of the destructiveness of these sprigs of nobility. The large dormitory is a coarse affair. I noticed a youngster at the farther end of it dressing, having, perhaps, overslept from the fatigues of the last night's rowing exertions.

As soon as we had despatched our breakfast we repaired to the castle again, and were conducted through its various wondrous apartments. Of the merits of these, our company entertained different opinions, — of their relative merits I mean. I believe the throne-room was the more generally admired. For myself, I know not with which apartment, as such, I was most pleased. But more than with any other single object or group of objects, I was delighted with the representation in marble of the death-scene of the Princess Charlotte.

Oh, what tales these walls could tell, had they but tongues! Of what scenes of pleasure and of misery have they not been witnesses! I am told the Queen is not now fond of Windsor as a residence.

The town of Windsor, as such, has little to interest

a stranger. The houses are small, old and dingy, the streets narrow and dirty, making one wonder how England's young and dainty Queen can endure to ride through them.

At about noon we set off for London by coach, riding along the great park, and for some distance the banks of the Thames. We entered this modern Babylon by Hyde Park.

I wondered I was not more excited on entering it. But my excitability had been already quite exhausted. "The bow cannot always be bent." We were set down at the "Saracen Inn," a dismal place enough. It was the stopping-place of the coach. Stage-coaches here do not, as with us in America, drive passengers about town. We all found accommodations at the same place, at Mr. Moore's, 6 Queen Street place, near Southwark bridge. Here we found several of our American acquaintances, among them Rev. Nathaniel Colver and Henry B. Stanton and wife, who had come to attend the convention.

I was pleased to find my landlord an intimate friend and warm admirer of George Thompson, who often stops here.

June 5. — I dropped in at the Somerset House, and handed my letter from Dr. W. to Mr. Robertson, the secretary of the Royal Society. He treated me politely, showing me the society's rooms and library, the book containing the members' autograph signatures, a telescope made by Sir Isaac Newton's own hands, and sundry other things fitted to excite my organ of veneration. The hall in which the society holds its meetings is hung with pictures by illustrious members. A meeting is to be held on next Thursday week, at which Mr. Robertson invited me to be present, promising to introduce me to various individuals distinguished for their attainments in science and literature.

June 7, Sunday. — We went first to St. Paul's, which is only a short distance from my lodgings. The service had just begun. The music of the organ and the chanting were excellent. The sermon I could not hear, but it was pronounced in a tone and manner monotonous and passionless. We soon left the chapel, and spent a few minutes in looking at the numerous monuments in the main body of the building. These are generally in honor of military and naval heroes. But this crowding of Christian temples with statues and other mementoes of warriors, what a commentary it is on the text, "Whosoever shall smite thee on thy right cheek, turn to him the other also"! From St. Paul's, of which I design a fuller examination hereafter, we proceeded to Westminster Abbey, intending also a glimpse only of this for the present.

The chapel door closed just as we entered, so that we could not hear the preacher. We sauntered awhile among the monuments in mute admiration of this wonderful pile of gothic architecture. Names familiar to the civilized world met our eyes on every side. On our way to the Abbey we passed the Queen's Horse Guards at their station. They are handsome fellows, and handsomely mounted on black horses. I have seen nothing equalling them. In St. James' Park we saw a detachment also of the

Queen's Foot Guards, marching to music which seemed quite an invasion of the Sabbath's sanctity. It is a lovely place, this St. James' Park. Large numbers were promenading here, enjoying its fresh air, its beautiful verdure, its pretty sheet of water, bearing on its glassy bosom numbers of birds, and its fine views of Buckingham and St. James' Palaces.

We resolved to get a glimpse of Pope's villa. We crossed the Thames in a boat, and soon found we had mistaken the distance; it was more than three miles; but anxious to see where Pope resided, we pushed on, although it was now quite sundown. Alas! how sadly I was disappointed! I saw but the place where Pope's villa had been, and hardly that. I was looking for a fine old cottage embosom-ed in luxuriant trees, and bright verdure, and many-colored flowers, and magnificent hedges; but found only an ugly wall of dingy brick and mortar, some ten feet high, and close upon the public road, itself narrow and full of dust! Oh, " what a falling off was there ! "

However, I tried to imagine, as well as I could, that hereabouts once lived the author of the " Essay on Man."

June 8. — Breakfasted with Joseph Pease, wife and daughter (Elizabeth). Mr. Pease is a Quaker of great wealth, and is at the bottom of the India movement, which he occupied some time in explain-ing to me. He showed me a letter he had lately re-ceived from Thomas Clarkson on the subject. Mr. Clarkson has high hopes of the movement. In the letter he says of O'Connell, who is likewise deeply interested in the cause of India, "He is a man after my own heart."

June 9. — At Greenwich. Greenwich is world-famous, as well for some other things as for its being made the starting-point so universally in the reckoning of longitude. The hospital is a noble charity. England, to her credit be it said, takes excellent care of her disabled and superannuated seamen, of whom several hundred are in this hospital, all of them, apparently, as happy as princes, weather-beaten though they seem, and mutilated and scarred as many of them are.

The chapel, which is a separate building, contains a picture of St. Paul's shipwreck, by our countryman, Benjamin West; for which, it is said, ten thousand pounds were paid.

The large picture gallery is filled with portraits of naval heroes, and representations of battles, and adorned with a multitude of banners, as trophies of British valor. Could not get admission into the observatory, the public being excluded from it. Its exterior exhibits nothing attractive. I thought of the efforts of the younger President Adams to establish a similar observatory at Washington.

That great statesman deemed it unworthy of his countrymen to measure longitude from Greenwich; but his efforts were unsuccessful.

Who has not heard of Greenwich fair? To see this was my principal object in visiting the place, and had I seen nothing else I should feel myself a hundred-fold rewarded for all my pains in the premises. My friend so managed the matter as to quite

startle me with a variety of novel impressions, by
keeping from me all knowledge of what was to come
till it met my observation.

Little occurred to raise my surprise until nightfall.
During the afternoon we were chiefly occupied with
observing sundry rural sports in the park. I observed
a colored woman walking arm in arm with a white
woman. In the New York park or on Boston Common such an occurrence would doubtless cause a
mob; but here it attracted no attention from any,
saving my American friend and myself. Distinctions
innumerable are there in England, and puerile enough
are the foundations of many of them; but I know of
none, and have heard of none, among them all, having
a foundation so utterly contemptible as that of the
great American aristocracy of color. The English
are too proud a people to tolerate for a moment the
existence of such a distinction. Ours will one day
be so.

At night it was a dazzling scene. I saw a play
which was a very *fair* one, to say the least. Entered
several of the halls where were refreshments and
music, and thousands of men and women richly
dressed. In one of these halls, which was some
hundreds of feet in length, we promenaded an hour.
Their marches, waltzes, jigs, jokes and tricks were
a caution to all true "knights of the sorrowful
figure." We left at eleven, the hour at which, by a
recent act of Parliament, — an act which unquestionably received many a malison this night, — such
entertainments must close, and got up to London by
the railroad at a little past midnight, glad enough

to have witnessed thus much of the Greenwich fair, which, from all accounts, was never so fully attended as on this occasion. "Never," says the London Times, "was it so crowded before. The steamers landed about 60,000 people, and the cars started every fifteen minutes and were always full. Forty steamers were employed, some taking from $1000 to $1400." And London is but one of many places whence people went to the fair.

June 9. — It having been intimated to Lord Brougham that the American delegation would be glad of an interview with him, his lordship signified that he would be happy to receive a limited number (because of his lordship's affliction in the loss of his mother and a daughter) of the delegates at his house this morning. Our object was twofold: we wished to see his lordship for our own personal gratification, and we wished to present to him a box made of remains of the Pennsylvania Hall, as an expression of the regard cherished by the American Abolitionists for his services in the cause of emancipation. The box was presented by Mr. Binney, who accompanied its presentation with pertinent remarks. Mr. Binney rose to offer his remarks, but at the request of his lordship delivered them sitting. His lordship's reply was happy, but incomparably less formal, more off-hand and business-like than the speech. He regretted very deeply his inability to attend the meetings of our convention; observing in a somewhat indignant tone that his enemies would misinterpret his absence, would infer from it a change of his opinion or a diminution of his interest in the cause;

whereas neither was ever so strong as it now is. I was quite surprised at his lordship's sensitiveness as to what might be said of him. Such sensitiveness in one who has been so long in public life is perhaps unusual, especially where, as in the present case, neither one's purse nor one's office can be affected by what is said. I am aware, however, that scarce anything would be more likely in England to mar a great man's reputation than to be thought opposed or indifferent to the cause of abolition.

I was introduced to Lord Brougham by one of whom his lordship is an especial admirer, George Thompson, whom our newspapers stigmatized as a "foreign renegado," and against whom our Boston "gentlemen of property and standing" got up a mob. The personal appearance of this great man is not at all prepossessing. It is un-English, but not *therefore* unprepossessing; or if it *be* English, it reminds one of the overworked and pale-faced operative, smarting under a sense of his wrongs and resolved that they shall be redressed, and not of the sleek ruddy-cheeked Englishman of the higher or the middle class. Like Cassius, his lordship has "a lean and hungry look." His person is erect, but rather below the average size. His head is above the average size, the knowing predominant over the reflective organs, but its frontal development is probably less than a phrenologist would infer *à priori*. His locality is very large, causality and comparison project over eventuality, which struck me as the smallest of his perceptive faculties. His hair, which appears to have been black, is fast turning gray, and is somewhat off at firmness and self-esteem.

His nervous-bilious temperament is prodigiously active. He was dressed very plainly. An American would probably be much more likely to suppose one of the liveried servants, who ushered us into the audience room, a nobleman than his lordship.

The furniture of the room in which we were received was also plain. There were two or three busts in marble, with Greek inscriptions on their pedestals. Subsequent to this interview, Joseph Sturge related to me the occasion of Lord Brougham's celebrated speech in the House of Lords touching West Indian slavery. Distinguished Abolitionists had often endeavored in vain to enlist his lordship's parliamentary exertions in behalf of its immediate and unconditional abolition.

Brougham could not adopt their plan, and was almost unwilling to hear it talked of. But at length he was prevailed on to favor Mr. John Scoble, who had just then returned from a tour of observation in the British West Indies, with an audience. Mr. Scoble entered into a detail of the evils and enormities of the slave system in those colonies. As Scoble proceeded, his lordship would occasionally utter an expression of surprise or of indignation. One instance of extreme cruelty had come under Mr. Scoble's own observation, and it was this : A woman, to expiate some offence, was placed on the treadmill, where, missing the step, her body dragged on the wheel, and was so horribly mangled that she soon died. An inquest was held upon the body. As Mr.

Scoble reached this point he was interrupted by his lordship, who, evidently quite agitated, inquired, "What was the verdict?" "Died by the visitation of God, my Lord," was the answer. Instantly, and as if moved by the shock of a galvanic battery, Brougham sprang to his feet, clenched his fists, and with a voice as loud and deep as his motions were energetic, exclaimed, "Horrible blasphemy! and I'll tell them so in the House!" A few hours afterwards his lordship made that famous speech which so electrified the British nation, on the subject of slavery in the West Indies.

Lord Brougham is not now the leader of a party. Cobbett once compared him to a duck, which having dived, no one could tell where it would come up. Perhaps the incident related above shows him liable to act from impulse, but it shows also that he has a heart. It is the general opinion that his lordship should have remained in the lower House, for which he has himself since leaving it expressed a preference.

I am told by Thompson that within the last few years his lordship's brain became so affected that he was obliged to cease for a twelvemonth from all business. It seemed to me as I sat listening to him, that he is not now out of danger from that source. Indeed, I marvel how any man could perform so much mental labor as he has done, and escape madness. I would go farther to see one Henry Brougham than a thousand Westminster Abbeys.

Called at the National Gallery with Wendell Phillips, in returning from Lord Brougham's. Several of Benjamin West's pictures are in the collection, but with all my patriotism I cannot fancy his portraits. Phillips, who is a connoisseur, pointed out several pictures which he thought unsurpassed by any of the kind he saw in Rome. The landscapes of Claude delighted me most.

June 11. — Westminster Hall is interesting chiefly, if not solely, from its associations. Within its walls have been poured forth the mightiest strains of forensic eloquence. It was here that the case of Warren Hastings was tried, in which Burke and Sheridan so distinguished themselves.

A large number — how many I do not now remember — of courts are now held here, several of which were in session to-day. The halls in which they are held resemble our New England school-rooms; the judge or judges sitting behind a table on a slightly elevated platform at one end of the hall, and the lawyers on parallel benches in front.

England's lawyers are as plentiful as the clergy of her Church "by law established." It is a striking analogy in the two professions, that both live by the sins of the people. In one of the courts I observed some fifty or sixty, sitting in their black gowns and big wigs. Serjeant Talfourd was among them, and made a few remarks while I was present. I should judge he must be eloquent when "warmed up." He is a handsome man, and I wondered how so literary a person should be able to keep so fresh a bloom upon his cheek. In America, a scholar, or even a lawyer, with so fresh and happy a countenance, would be deemed a universal marvel. In England, it is a thing

to be expected rather than marvelled at.   The gowns
and formidable wigs worn by the judges and lawyers
here are supposed to impart dignity to the administration of justice, as similar disfigurements of the
bishops and clergy are thought to inspire veneration
for religion.

Of Westminster Abbey I will say, the impressions
it made on my mind were not so overwhelming as
those it has made on other minds, or even as I should
at one time have anticipated.   Webster is said to
have declared that on his mind it made an impression which he should never forget.   Few who have
seen the Abbey would find it difficult to say as much.
I would not for a great deal have missed seeing this
grand specimen of gothic architecture, this magnificent receptacle of a portion of Briton's illustrious
dead.   They would not have it desecrated by a
monument of Byron.   Oh the hypocrites !

June 12. — The " World's Convention " met at an
early hour in "Freemasons' Hall," a noble place,
worthy of such a meeting.

The chair was taken by Thomas Clarkson, who,
taking up the negro's cause at the age of twenty-
four, has advocated it, through evil and through
good report, for the last fifty-seven years.   He was
introduced to the convention by Joseph Sturge, who
had previously requested the audience to abstain
from all applause during his presence, remarking
that when some years since "our dear friend" visited
London, and received "the freedom of the city," he
suffered greatly from the excitement of the occasion.
Mr. Clarkson's daughter-in-law sat beside him with

his grandson, who was also introduced to the convention by Mr. Sturge, with the remark that he is nine years old to-day, and the only one bearing the name of his venerable ancestor Clarkson. The convention were quite affected, and tears were in the eyes of many.

The president *read* his speech to the convention, and with a great deal of fervor.

While Clarkson was reading his speech there entered the hall one of the noblest-looking personages I ever looked upon, and took a seat just at my left elbow. I perceived it was with the greatest difficulty that the convention abstained from applauding. I at once concluded it must be Daniel O'Connell, and soon found my conclusion a correct one. It was a feast to look on him; and when, as the president took his seat, he rose to address the convention, I felt quite like going into ecstasies.

The great "agitator" is all that I expected, and more. His person is uncommonly large, erect, and of admirable proportions, while his feet and hands are of very aristocratic dimensions.

His voice is exceedingly rich and of great compass and flexibility. Its tones fall on the car like notes of sweetest music, or the thunder of a tremendous cataract, just as he pleases or as best comports with his subject. Something of the Irish brogue it of course has, but that makes it all the richer. To look at him as he sat listening to Clarkson's speech, one would hardly deem him the agitator he is. There is such an expression of placidity, of cheerfulness, of a mind at ease with itself, in his ample, roseate countenance, that one can scarce help feeling happy in the observation of it.

Yet in that mild face are muscles capable of playing all the variations of the soul, and we all had occasion to admire the demonstration of these capabilities, made in his speech this morning, especially in that part of it in which he paid his respects to our republican slaveholders and their apologists. He evidently thinks on his legs, and his easy, off-hand manner of speaking is delightful. The speech just alluded to was full of power and beauty. It was, too, spontaneous, and showed its author to possess such a commanding influence over the nobler sentiments of our nature as I hardly expected to find even in O'Connell. His head is of a magnitude proportionate to that of his body; the forehead is very massive, worthy of a phrenologist's admiration.

Mr. O'Connell having made a complimentary allusion to Massachusetts, I was urged by Wendell Phillips to respond to it. It was the best opportunity I ever had of showing my littleness.

June 13. — O'Connell advocated the resolution calling on Christians to consider if they are not bound to refuse to fellowship slaveholders *as Christians.* Several clergymen objected to its adoption, that it would be an interference with the right of the churches to fix their own conditions of Christian communion. Mr. O'Connell, who is a Roman Catholic, could assure the convention that the church to which *he* belonged would be glad of an expression of the opinion on this subject of so respectable a body as the convention.

June 14, *Sunday.* —The Queen and Prince Albert were to worship in the royal chapel of St. James. A seat is reserved in the chapel for foreigners, I was told, but dreading the tedious mechanism of the church service, and uncertain if I should be able to hear the sermon, I made no attempt to go in, preferring to stand, just before the conclusion of the service, in front of the palace gate through which the Queen was to pass on leaving the chapel. I found this a favorable position for viewing her person as she passed. She looks better than I had supposed, is, indeed, a bright, buoyant, buxom lass.

The Prince looks still better, has a fine form, a handsome forehead and very classical features. He presided at the great Anti-slavery meeting in Exeter Hall the other day, and made a very sensible speech. A few brief moments were all that we saw them, and my attention was quite confined to the Queen. The engravings of her give a good idea of her appearance ; but hers is a face that suffers in being lithographed, as one of an inferior complexion gains by the process. The Queen was shot at as she was driving near Constitution Hill, on the evening of the 6th instant. This of course created great excitement. The man who perpetrated the act is supposed to have been insane ; some think the pistol was leadless. The two Houses of Parliament have waited on her with congratulations on her providential preservation. The clergy are getting ready to thank God for it, and are waiting only for the Archbishop of Canterbury to furnish them with a set of words in which to offer up their thanks. "A wonderful interposition

of Providence!" exclaims almost every one you
meet. Yet I suppose if a beggar girl had escaped
unscathed the discharge of a pistol loaded with
something besides powder, it would scarce occur to
any one that there was any Providence in the
matter.

June 15. — At the convention O'Connell delivered
a glorious speech touching the question of granting
compensation for cargoes of human beings liberated
by being cast within the jurisdiction of Great Britain;
and he handled without gloves the resolutions of Mr.
Calhoun in the United States Senate on that subject.
He paid his respects again to the American Abolitionists, whom, especially the women among them, he
complimented in the highest strains. I spoke at
some length on the importance of enlisting the literature of Europe in the cause of abolition.

June 16. — Dr. Bowring made a speech on "Slavery
in the East," from which I inferred that Mahomet-
ans are much better Christians than most of my own
countrymen.

June 17. — Breakfasted in Cecil Street with a company of true spirits from Ireland; namely, Richard
Allen and Richard D. Webb, with their wives,
brothers, sisters, &c. They are Quakers. I learned
from them that O'Connell's income as a lawyer could
not have been less than seven thousand pounds a
year at the time he consented to go into Parliament;
that the "O'Connell rent," his present means of
support, averages about eleven thousand pounds per
annum, which he expends in agitation and the support

of his family, keeping himself all the while a poor man.

Garrison, Rogers, Remond and Adams arrived this afternoon.

June 18. — Dined with Thomas Sturge, who is a cousin of Joseph Sturge.

June 19. — To breakfast with Dr. Bowring was a treat. Messrs. Cremineux, Isambert, Judge Jeremie and Garrison were present. A beautiful daughter of the Doctor's presided at the table. Their residence, 1 Queen Square, Westminster, is a pleasant location. Near it Milton and Addison, and the great Utilitarian philosopher, Jeremy Bentham, lived and died. The house of the last was shown me from a window of Dr. Bowring's study. Bentham died in Bowring's arms, leaving the latter his executor. It was delightful to hear the devoted pupil talk of his great master, and I thought it pleasant to the former to have so glad a listener. We were some time in the study by by ourselves, having left the company around the breakfast table ; and the Doctor gave me a lock of Bentham's hair, and also a note addressed to him in the handwriting of Sir Samuel Romilly, one of his strong friends and admirers. I received from him a letter of introduction to Dr. T. Southward Smith, to whom Bentham bequeathed his body to be used in illustration of the science of anatomy.

June 20. — Campbell the poet made a speech at the convention to-day, imploring literary men, especially those of America, to write on the subject of slavery. "If they can show it to be right," said he, "*in the devil's name let them do so.*" But he was equally anxious that American writers should write in prose, for among them were some of the best prose-writers in the world, while their poetry went on all-fours.

Stanton, who followed the poet, spoke of him as having intimated that we in America *have* no poets; when Campbell immediately interrupted him with the exclamation, "No, no, I did not say America has *no* poets. Bryant is a noble poet." I supposed Campbell did not mean to hit our poets quite so hard. He was evidently much agitated and embarrassed, being unaccustomed to address public bodies. In person, Thomas Campbell is below the average size, yet there is in that finely developed forehead, smooth as polished marble, and in that dark sparkling eye, something which tells you at once that the possessor is no ordinary mortal.

June 27. — This was the last day of the convention. Spoke on the question of holding another similar convention at some future period.

A deal of unpleasant feeling has been produced by the exclusion from the convention of the women delegates from America. The roll of the convention was made out by the committee of the British and Foreign Anti-slavery Society, who seem to have had quite exclusively the management of all its proceedings, and in that roll the names of those women were omitted. On the first day of its sessions, Wendell Phillips moved the appointment of a committee to prepare a roll of the convention, maintaining that it was the province of the convention alone to determine who should be in it as members.

This caused considerable fluttering and a protracted debate. Dr. Bowring and William Ashurst took noble ground, and defended (to their praise be it recorded) the claims of our women with great zeal. So also did George Thompson, who utterly demolished the objections to their admission urged by Rev. Mr. Burnett. I, of course, maintained as well as I could in so short a space, the rights of the women. O'Connell was not present, but on my introducing to him Mr. Garrison, the day after his arrival, and Mr. Garrison having alluded to the exclusion of the women, he exclaimed, "It was a cowardly sacrifice of principle to a vulgar prejudice."

Soon after Mr. Garrison's arrival the question was again introduced by Wendell Phillips in another form (his original motion having been defeated by a very large majority). Mr. Phillips was again defeated. A protest was then drawn up by Prof. Adam, giving a brief account of our views of the convention's proceedings in relation to the whole matter, and this afternoon a motion was made to enter it on the journal of the convention. On this motion a spirited debate ensued, but it was, at length, laid upon the table. This I deemed the most oppressive act of the convention, and denounced it as an act which the most thorough-paced slaveholders in America would have been ashamed to perpetrate.

The protest was signed by a goodly number comprised of Englishmen, Scotchmen and Irishmen, as well as Americans. O'Connell was not present at this debate. In addressing the convention upon this question, I said I had hoped that the vote would be taken without discussion; that here in a World's

Convention, there would be very little difference of opinion on the subject, how much soever Englishmen, as such, might differ from some of us respecting it. We have been told that when the invitation was issued no reference was made to women. But I ask if, when that invitation was sent into different quarters of the globe, it was not intended to make this in reality a World's Convention of Abolitionists —that Abolitionists everywhere should be represented in it. Will any one undertake to say that it was intended to exclude from representation in this body the Abolitionists of Massachusetts and of Pennsylvania? for it is not true, as some one has asserted, that Massachusetts is the only State that has sent women delegates hither. Do you intend to say that the Abolitionists of those States had not the right to elect such persons as they pleased to represent them in this convention? But you do say this if you exclude from these seats any whom those Abolitionists have regularly appointed to occupy them. I cannot, I will not, believe that the committee of the British and Foreign Anti-slavery Society did intend thus to tie up the hands of American Abolitionists.

And what a misnomer to call this a *World's* Convention of Abolitionists, where some of the oldest and most thoroughgoing Abolitionists in the world are denied the right to be represented in it by delegates of their own choice! The Massachusetts Anti-slavery Society would have *spurned* the invitation of the committee had it known it was not at liberty to elect its own delegates. The members of that society are none of your half-and-half sort of Abolitionists.

They are thoroughly imbued with love for the cause;
have made sacrifices for it; have been ready, I trust,
to die for it if need were; and they know it were as
contradictory of facts, as it would be ungrateful, to
say that women, in virtue of their sex, were unquali-
fied to represent them in a convention of this character. Let it not be forgotten that this was designed
to be a World's Convention. The invitation was
extended to all Abolitionists throughout the world;
and no doubt it was earnestly desired, as well as designed, that they should all be represented here. If
this were not the grand prominent idea of the committee, I know not what it was. I know that some-
time after the invitation was sent forth, and after
some of our delegates had been appointed, a letter
was published by some one, stating that gentlemen
only were expected to attend. But we neither did
nor could regard this as of any consequence. We
deemed the question of who should sit in the convention would be determined by the convention itself;
not by any self-constituted committee, and least of
all, by any individual. But we are now told that it
would be outraging the tastes, habits, customs and
prejudices of the English people to allow women to
sit in this convention. I have a great respect for
the customs of Old England. But I ask, gentlemen,
if it be right to set up the customs and habits, not to
say prejudices, of Englishmen as a standard for the
government on this occasion of Americans, and of
persons belonging to several other independent nations? It seems to me that it were, to say the least,
very unadvisable to do so. I can see neither reason

nor policy in so doing. Besides, I deprecate *the principle* of this objection. In America it would exclude from our conventions all persons of color, for there, customs, habits, tastes, prejudices, would be outraged by *their* admission. And I do not wish to be deprived of the aid of those who have done so much for our cause, for the purpose of gratifying any mere custom or prejudice. I know that women have furnished most essential aid in accomplishing what has been accomplished in the State of Massachusetts. If, in the Legislature of that State, I have been able to do anything in furtherance of this cause, by keeping on my feet eight or ten hours day after day, it was mainly owing to the valuable assistance I derived from the *women* of Massachusetts. And shall such women be denied seats in this convention? My friend, George Thompson yonder, can testify to the faithful services rendered to this cause by some of those same women. He can tell you that when "gentlemen of property and standing," in broad day and in broadcloth, undertook to drive him from the city of Boston, putting his life in peril, it was our women who made their own persons a bulwark of protection around him! And shall such women be refused seats here in a convention seeking the emancipation of slaves throughout the world? I was sorry to hear my friend from Pennsylvania say that he was satisfied with the explanation which had been given, that we ought to understand the invitation in the sense in which it has been said to have been understood by the committee. I object to acting on any such understanding of it, because, as was well observed by another, it would be taking the English yardstick to measure the American mind.

And as to its being a sin against God to allow women to participate in the proceedings of a body like this, I confess I was astonished to hear such a sentiment uttered here, for this is neither the time nor the place to discuss *that* question. Another friend from America has said that there is a difference of opinion *there* on this subject; that the American delegates themselves were not united respecting it; and that the great body of the American people were utterly opposed to the admission of women into such companies as this. I admit it. But I have to ask that friend if he means to say that the great body of the real working Abolitionists of America would be opposed to it. I know they would *not*. In America women have taken, and they continue to take, part in meetings of this sort. On the American Anti-slavery platform they stand as the equals of the men in respect, at least, of rights and privileges. The American Anti-slavery Society has decided that as members of that body they ought so to stand. It has been so decided in most of the local societies in Massachusetts, where the standard of abolitionism was first planted. And with all deference to the Abolitionists present, I say that the best, the bravest, and those who have sacrificed most for this cause, are with very few exceptions decidedly on this side of the question; and they would never have consented to any participation in the proceedings of this or of any other convention had they supposed that any delegates freely chosen by themselves would be

denied the right to sit in it.   Some one has said that
if women are admitted they will take sides on this
question.   Well, what then?   Have they not just as
good right to take sides as we have?   But I shall be
satisfied if this convention, not the committee, will
decide who are and who are not entitled to seats
here.   This will also, I doubt not, satisfy the delegates whose seats are contested.   They do not feel at
liberty — I speak of those more especially who have
come from Massachusetts — to withhold their credentials from the convention, merely because a committee
not created by this body has seen fit to reject them.
They feel bound in justice to those by whom they
were sent to impose the responsibility of receiving
or of rejecting those credentials upon the convention
itself.   They therefore present them in obedience
to their convictions of duty.   You gentlemen can
dispose of them as you please.

SECOND SPEECH.

I agree with my friend Mr. Stanton, who has preceded me, that great ignorance prevails in America
as to the proceedings and sentiments of those in this
country who advocate the abolition of the slave trade
and of slavery.   I doubt, however, if real ignorance
on these points is so general as he has given you
reason to suppose.   Many know the truth well
enough, but are not willing to acknowledge it.
They also know their duty in the premises, but are
not willing to do it.   There are others — and
it is not a small class either — on our side of
the water who have heard of but have not re-

membered the doctrines and doings of the British Abolitionists. They have heard them explained often enough, and for the time being were well-enough satisfied of their soundness, but have straightway forgotten all about the matter. They are much like a good old woman with whom a metaphysical friend of mine was wont to converse on the philosophy of sugar. He used to tell her that sugar of itself was not sweet; that that quality in it which we call sweetness was but a certain sensation produced by the action of certain particles of matter peculiarly organized, upon the nerves of feeling. This explanation when given was always quite clear to the good woman; yet at the very next time of meeting my friend, she would always exclaim, "Well, I believe sugar *is* sweet after all." To persons of this sort, the facts and opinions in relation to the anti-slavery enterprise must needs be often repeated to be fully impressed on their understandings. And in no way can this be more effectually done, whether in respect of this or of any other class of persons opposed to our cause through ignorance or otherwise, than by the constant iteration and reiteration of those facts and opinions through the medium of the numerous periodical and other publications of Great Britain.

It has been said that in America we are fond of titles, and that we have a vast number of D.D.'s. Perhaps it is so, and the prevalence of the latter may be accounted for from a simple fact. The theology of America — I mean of the slaveholding part of the country — is made to sanction slavery, to teach that slavery is an ordinance of God. And need it be said that a system of divinity which sanctions such a complication of abominations as that of American slavery must needs be sick, and therefore in need of doctors? There are certain points on which it strikes me, if I may throw out the suggestion here, that the able reviews of this country might enlarge with great profit to the cause in which we are engaged. I refer to the gross inconsistencies in which slavery involves Americans. Let their practices be tried by their avowed theory, — the theory which is blazoned forth to the world in the preamble of our Declaration of Independence. That theory has been alluded to more than once here to-day. Professedly, ours is a republican government. And what is the great idea of a republic? Is it not this, that "governments derive their just powers from the consent of the governed," and that they should be administered for the benefit of *the whole people?* Wherein does this differ from the idea of an autocracy? Is it not chiefly in this, that the head of an autocracy professes to derive his power to govern, not from the consent of the governed, but directly from the Almighty? The autocrat, not less than the republican, owns that government should be administered for the good of the public.

I undertake to say that the autocracy of Russia, in its practical operation, is not wider of the true idea of a republic than is the government of our country. Is it not indeed a mockery to call that a republic in which one sixth of the population are held in chains?

We have declared to the world that "all men are created equal; that they are endowed by their Creator with certain inalienable rights; that among these

are life, liberty, and the pursuit of happiness." This
is our theory. What is our practice? We tread on
the necks of nearly three millions of men, and buy
and sell them like brute beasts in the shambles. I
have been told that this horrible inconsistency was
felt so forcibly by one of our Fourth-of-July orators,
that on reading the Declaration, he attempted to get
rid of it, by a certain interpolation. "All men," said
he, "are created equal, *except niggers.*" And this is
probably the meaning attached to the instrument by
thousands who do not choose, like the Fourth-of-July
orator, to express the exception. Take another of
our inconsistencies : We have declared in the Constitution of the United States that there shall be no
abridgment of the freedom of the press. Yet we
have not, practically, as you have been told to-day,
freedom of the press in America. Even in the national Legislature, a law was proposed, and passed
one branch of it, to prevent the circulation through
the public mails of all documents containing the
"self-evident truths" of our own Declaration of Independence.

The law proposed to give power to postmasters to
rifle the mail-bags, and commit such documents to
the flames. And not only have the circulations of the
productions of the ·press in· many parts of our country been prevented, and the prevention attempted to
be enforced by a law of Congress, but presses themselves have been broken up with impunity, at an expense too, in one instance at least, of human life.
In such a state of things, what folly to pretend there
is, or can be, "liberty of the press"! Ours is claimed

to be the only, or almost the only, country in which perfect freedom of religious opinion is enjoyed.

We boast that the pilgrim fathers of our land braved the dangers of the broad Atlantic, and the still greater dangers of the then savage wilderness of the Western world, that they might establish, and transmit unimpaired to their posterity, this inestimable blessing. Yet we have *no* religious liberty in America. For what *is* religious liberty? It is not simply the liberty to think; for the greatest tyrant that ever breathed could not prevent a solitary individual from thinking, if he chose to think.

It implies something more. It implies liberty of expression. This liberty we do not possess in America. The grand object, therefore, in the pursuit of which our fathers abandoned the shores of Old England, and incurred so many hazards and hardships, has not yet been accomplished.

A man may not, in one half of America, utter his religious convictions on the subject of slavery, unless, forsooth, those convictions chance to be that that institution is a "patriarchial" one.

And yet we are boasting constantly of our religious liberty, and of our liberty of the press.

Was there ever a greater inconsistency?

In the Constitution of the United States it is solemnly guaranteed "that the citizens of each State shall be entitled to all privileges and immunities of citizens in the several States." Yet, notwithstanding this solemn provision of the Constitution, the citizen of a free State having a colored skin, no sooner sets his foot on the soil of a slave State than he is robbed of all his "privileges and immunities," and reduced to the condition of an article of merchandise. As I have remarked on a former occasion, thousands of robberies of this description are perpetrated annually in the slave States of America, and they are sanctioned by legal enactments of the Legislatures of those States. A friend of mine, some two or three years since, in walking the streets of New Orleans, fell in with six or eight free colored persons, some of whom had been in his own employment in the State of New York. They were in chain gangs; that is, gangs of persons employed on the public roads, each with a ball chained to his leg.

They were to be continued in that situation for twelve months from the time of entering it, and, if not previously able to *prove*, by the testimony of a white man, that they were not brutes, that they were freemen, to be sold into perpetual bondage. My friend, being a liberal man, obtained their release, but it was at considerable expense. This is but a single instance of thousands of cases which, I have already said, occur in my own country annually. And these terrible outrages upon the rights of our free colored citizens, sanctioned by slaveholding statutes, are in palpable violation of the letter of the Constitution of the United States. But these kidnapping statutes of the slave States in general, atrocious as they are, are exceeded in atrocity by one enacted a little more than a year since by the Legislature of the State of Alabama, and which, I believe, has been referred to by Mr. Binney.

By the former, the colored man who had proved freedom by the requisite evidence, and paid the expenses of his arrest, was permitted to return to his family; but by the latter, even from the first moment of its enactment, any scoundrel within the limits of Alabama might seize upon a free person of color found there, and reduce him to irremediable and perpetual slavery. They will not allow him the wretched privilege of proving his freedom, paying the charges and taking his own body away. When the fact of the passing of this law was communicated to me, I chanced to be addressing the Legislature of my own native State. I did not hesitate to say in my place, that if all the demons of perdition had been let loose upon the earth and formed into a legislature, it would have been impossible for them to have perpetrated so great an outrage upon the inalienable rights of humanity; for, according to the doctrines of demonology, devils, even, are not permitted to lay violent hands upon innocent men. But in addition to all this legal kidnapping — made legal by slaveholding legislators, but *il*-legal by the paramount law, the Constitution of the land — there is not a little carried on which, with what some will perhaps deem a strange inconsistency, is condemned by the laws of slaveholding States themselves. The slaveholding power, legal or illegal, stretches its long claws even into the free States, and clutches children from the very hearthstones of their free parents, hurries them off clandestinely to the slave States, and sells them into everlasting bondage. And the cases of this illegal stealing of children for the slave shambles of the South are neither few nor far between. Such are a few of the enormous, wicked inconsistencies in which slavery involves the republicans of North America. Let them be seized and treated as they deserve to be by the literary men and women of Great Britain.

Let them be held up in your newspapers, in your great reviews and other publications, to the hatred of all Europe, aye, to the execration of the civilized world! And while you spare not these or any other abominable inconsistencies, I would beseech you to be merciful as you can to their pseudo-republican authors. I hope that the periodicals of Great Britain will also take some pains to hold up in their true light certain persons in America who call themselves Abolitionists, but who never *do* anything for the cause, except to find fault with its active friends. In the free States almost every man will now say that he is an Abolitionist; but many who say so will at the same time take great care to condemn our measures if not our doctrines, and all, or nearly all, who are *doing* anything for the cause, and are, in fact, among the worst enemies against whom we have to do. They *call* themselves Abolitionists and profess to feel deeply for the perishing bondman, because they do not wish to avow themselves so utterly hostile to liberty and humanity as a direct acknowledgment of the fact would proclaim them to be. But a few days before I came to this country, on meeting one of this sort of Abolitionists, I said to him, "Sir, did you ever hear the story of the boy and the calf? I will tell it to you. An intelligent boy was looking at a calf in the

presence of his father. 'Father,' inquired the lad,
'calling the tail one, how many legs would the calf
have?' 'Why, my son,' replied the father, 'that is
a very simple question; it would have five, to be sure.'
'Not at all,' rejoined the lad, 'not at all, father: *calling* the tail a leg would not make it one.'" So my
friends, let us say to this sort of Abolitionists, calling
yourselves Abolitionists will not *make* you such.
[Some in the audience not understanding the anecdote, requested Mr. B. to repeat it; Mr. B. said:] I
dislike to repeat an anecdote to the same audience.
But I will give you another, equally applicable, perhaps, to the same sort of persons.

They remind me of the good old woman's son John.
"My son John," she said, "is the most tender-hearted boy I ever knew: ask him to pick up a basket of
chips, and he'll cry."

The Abolitionists in question are also very tender-
hearted; they feel deeply for the poor slave, and are
especially concerned lest his cause should be injured
by the overwrought zeal and earnestness of its principal advocates; but the moment you ask one of them
to *do* something himself for the cause, why, like John,
he begins to complain, begins to "cry." We call on
Englishmen to "come over and help us" convert these
tender-hearted Abolitionists to a sense of the importance of *doing* something for the slave's deliverance.
We do not urge you to come in person, but come to
us in the columns of your daily press, in the pages
of your books, of your novels and romances even;
in your poetry and in your noble reviews, which are

read and reverenced in every town and village throughout the length and breadth of our whole land.

I desire especially that our British friends will labor to produce such an impression on *the clergy* of our country as will induce them to act in behalf of humanity. We often have British clergymen visiting our country. These, though good Abolitionists here, have usually, it grieves me to say, left their abolitionism at home on going to America, or have been induced by their brethren on the other side of the water to keep quiet on the subject; so that our pro-slavery enemies have quoted them against us, and they have really supported the atrocious system of slavery by withholding their testimony against it. The inference usually drawn from their course among us is this, that there the British clergy are no more than the American in favor of emancipation; for if they were, it has been said they would unite with the Abolitionists, and lift up their voice against slavery.

Let it be so no longer. And I beseech you to send forth by your own clergy crossing the water the voice of earnest, affectionate remonstrance, both against slavery and against the awful silence respecting it by the clergy of America.

THIRD SPEECH.

In regard to the next World's Convention, proposed to be held in America, I think it would be peculiarly unfortunate if a convention for the abolition of slavery throughout the world were to be called in America by the British and Foreign Anti-slavery Society. The Americans, like those of every other nation, have their national pride and their national prejudices; and I know that if such a call were sent forth from such a quarter, it would excite in many men that pride and those prejudices. For this reason I hope that the amendment will be adopted. I doubt not that two years hence there will have been such a change in the public sentiment of our country as will warrant abundantly the assembling there of a convention similar to this. Those who have spoken upon the affairs of America have dwelt upon the dark side of the picture. I know that this has been peculiarly the case with myself. It has been a picture of blackness which has been hung up for the contemplation of this assembly. But there is also a bright side of the picture. There has been a great change brought about in the public sentiment of America relative to slavery. It is only some eight or ten years since that there was throughout the length and breadth of that mighty land but one solitary voice * lifted up in denunciation of the giant crime of our nation. But since then there have been joined to it, I might say hundreds of thousands of other voices. And there was at that period but one publication † which would venture to speak out in behalf of the truths emblazoned in the preamble of the American Declaration of Independence. I remember that one of the first numbers of that publication casually fell into my hands, and on looking over its pages and seeing the announcement of the mighty purpose it proposed to accomplish, and

---

* That of William Lloyd Garrison.
† The Liberator.

especially when my eye rested on a sentence to this effect, that the editor would tell scorners that that little sheet should yet cause that mighty nation to shake from its centre to its circumference, I flung down the paper with this exclamation, that the editor must either be a knave or a fool. It was not till some time afterwards that I took an active interest in this cause. And if I have been able to do anything in America, especially as a legislator, in behalf of the inalienable rights of humanity, I may say with truth that the original occasion of my acting at all in the premises was my hearing the distinguished individual who now sits before me in this house, — George Thompson. I had prejudices against the Abolitionists at that time. I considered them a set of hairbrained fanatics, who, to accomplish their object, would scarce scruple to dismember the Union, to get up a servile war, and excite the slaves to "cut their masters' throats ;" and it was only by the urgent solicitations of a personal friend that I consented one Fourth of July to go and hear the eloquent orator to whom I have just alluded.

I was astonished to hear him say, and to find the sentiment sanctioned by other Abolitionists and by the American Society of Abolitionists, that so far from disturbing the country and exciting the slaves to mutiny, he would not, with all his love of liberty, injure the hair of a slaveholder's head to liberate every slave in the universe, for he would not, he said, do evil that good might come. But I had not listened long to the orator's eloquence before my prejudices began to melt away like fairy frostwork

before the sun.   My own experience has been essentially that of thousands of individuals in America.
As light has been disseminated over the land and the people instructed on this subject, a change has been going on in the opinions of our countrymen.   Now, instead of there being only a single press devoted to the advocacy of this cause, there are large numbers of presses and hundreds of thousands of individuals enlisted in its behalf.

Indeed, when I consider the weight of prejudice, of ignorance, and of opposition, against which the Abolitionist cause in America has had to contend, I cannot but think its progress has been truly wonderful, greater by far than its most sanguine friends could have reasonably anticipated.   Two years hence it will have extended its progress so far that a World's Anti-slavery Convention may well be assembled in America.   In Massachusetts, where five years ago, even in its capital, our headquarters of liberality, of benevolence, and of refinement, a few women could not meet to pray for the slave lest they were mobbed; where Garrison, the originator of the whole abolition movement in America, for attempting to unite in the prayers of those devoted women, was dragged through the streets with a rope round his neck, and thrust into a jail for safe-keeping; where such men as Follen, Channing and May could not be heard before a legislative committee; and where, even, at a still later period, the Abolitionists were driven to hold their meetings in a barn, — it is now not only safe, it is even held honorable, to speak out plainly in behalf of the outraged rights of the negro.   I rejoice in this change.

It makes me think better of my country. And although I am there denied the right of locomotion — cannot travel southwardly three days without endangering my life, yet I can say most heartily of my country, what your noble Cowper said of yours, "O America! with all thy faults, I love thee still." And let me add, that my country has never seemed so dear to me as since I have been in England. I have a great veneration for England and the English. I thank them, in the name of the down-trodden slave, in the name of humanity, and in the name of the God of humanity and of mercy, for their beneficent exertions in the glorious cause of emancipation.

But I love America and the Americans *more;* and it is *because* I love them that I have in this convention denounced so freely the atrocities perpetrated by American slaveholders and sanctioned by their apologists. It would give me great pleasure to see a convention of the Abolitionists of the world assembled in America. And should a convention be called there, I hope it will be, in reality, a *World's* Convention, a convention in which every friend of humanity, duly delegated, will be heartily welcomed to a seat *without respect of color, of creed, or of sex.*

The soirée which was gotten up in fine style by our British friends at the "Crown and Anchor Tavern," distinguished of old as the resort of such men as Fox, Pitt, Sheridan, &c., may be considered as the *finale* of our "World's Convention" anti-slavery proceedings, one grand parting meeting. Stanton made the first speech. He was followed by M. Duclos de Boussais in a very brief speech.　Next came Garrison, who talked of " Woman's Rights " — blaming the convention for its disregard of them — of universal suffrage in Ireland, and the necessity of a universal language.

George Thompson read an appropriate poem, written for the occasion by Dr. Beattie.　Mrs. Mott spoke briefly and beautifully.　Mr. Remond also made a short speech.

CHAPTER V.

EXTRACTS FROM "REMINISCENCES OF A FLYING TRIP"
TO PARIS, ENGLAND, SCOTLAND AND IRELAND.

MY departure for Paris has been somewhat de-
layed by sitting to Haydon. This great artist
has undertaken a picture of the convention under
the "patronage" of the London committee. I understand it will occupy him a twelvemonth.* A
small portion, only, of the portraits are intended to
be likenesses. Of these, sketches were made, each
on a separate canvas, during the sitting of the convention, to be transferred to the large piece, the
artist occupying for that purpose a room adjoining
Freemasons' Hall, so that the favored members could
visit him at his convenience. These sketches were
subsequently purchased by the Duchess of Sutherland. My protracted stay in London has enabled
me to give Mr. H. a few sittings more. I tell him
he has given it a look of too much severity or sharp-
ness. He calls it, with one of his significant expressions of countenance, "a revolutionary look."
Perhaps he fancied I must have felt somewhat "revolutionary," in making some of my speeches in Freemasons' Hall. I am to give him another sitting on

* This picture a friend of ours, of Melrose, Mrs. H. E. Page, saw last summer at the National Gallery of Portraits at Kensington; and although she
had not heard of its existence, she at once recognized Mr. Bradburn's portrait
taken forty-two years before.

my return from Paris. The time chosen by the
artist is that of the delivery of Clarkson's speech.
If appeals to one's love of approbation could relieve
the tedium of sitting, I take it Haydon's sitters find
frequent relief. I felt I should like to stand behind
the door and hear how he would talk to other sitters.
Barring this flattering propensity of his, which is
very non-characteristic of an Englishman, I should
judge Haydon to be a fine specimen of a John Bull.
We were speaking of French and English characteristics. Some allusion of mine to the soldiers of the
two nations led Haydon to say, "The French are
light physically, as they are frivolous mentally.
They are good for rapid marches. They *charge*
well, but have not the substance and firmness of the
English to *stand* a charge. They can live on almost
nothing, wanting little but bread. The English sol-
dier *must* have his beef. A pint of our beer would
abolish a Frenchman."

Dined to-day with M. E. Duclos de Boussais,
one of the French delegates to the convention. He
once edited a paper in France, and is under a sort
of expatriation for political heresies. He is a very
zealous republican, and doubts little that republicanism will be established here in France on the
death of Louis Phillippe. He denounces Napoleon
as an infamous tyrant and hypocrite. M. de B.
offers me letters to his wife, who is still in Paris. I
was called on at the dinner table for a speech, which
I concluded with this sentiment: "The friends of
freedom throughout the world." My French friend
spoke with a deal of enthusiasm.

July 12. — Leave to-day for Paris. Went on board the beautiful steamer "Phœnix," between seven and eight A.M. M. Duclos de Boussais came to see me off, bringing me letters and never so many kind wishes. He introduced me to the captain, who is a Frenchman.

My American fellow-traveller, Col. Jonathan P. Miller, of Vermont, was "on hand," and very soon the steamer was ploughing her way down the winding Thames amid myriads of vessels of every description, and beneath a sky as beautifully sunny as one often sees in England. The English are proud of their Thames. But to an American there is nothing wonderful about it. He is impressed chiefly by its utility. I have followed it from Windsor to its mouth now.

Arrived at Havre at 8 A.M. As we entered the harbor it reminded me of Nantucket. The town did not impress me very pleasantly. I have been told by some American friends here — the Winslows — that the suburbs are very delightful. Saw an American ship leaving port with hundreds of emigrants on board. Her beautiful "star-spangled banner," as it streamed in the breeze and glittered in the sunlight, *would* remind me of Campbell's withering yet just apostrophe to our national flag. Our companions in the diligence to Rouen were a young lad and an Englishman, both taciturn. But their taciturnity was compensated by the volubility of the Colonel, who remarked on almost everything that we passed, — about sects and parties, in both religion and politics, — giving us the dimensions of sundry great men and

small, — Daniel Webster, Louis Philippe and Berna-
dotte among them; recounted with pride as well as
enthusiasm his own seeings and doings "in the four
quarters of the globe," — interspersing the whole with
sundry passages of poetry from Byron and others,
full of fire and of eulogy of "noble deeds and daring
high," and accompanying the recitations with a su-
perabundance of gestures, doubtless the more animated from recollections of his own military exploits
in Greece. Our course to Rouen was along the
banks of the Seine. The Colonel, who is lame, did
not accompany me in my rambles about the place.
The scenery hereabout is picturesque, almost approaching the grand, some of it. But I wished to
push on to "all France," as some one has called Paris.
I see a hundred things in France to one in "Old England," to remind me of America. The sky, the earth,
its cultivation, the people, the animals, all look more
American than any I have before seen since leaving
home. And herein have I been disappointed. I
fancied we and our country resembled in outward
aspect the English more than the French, yet I notice here things strikingly dissimilar to aught among
us. The buildings of the villages through which we
pass are of a dirty-looking material, a sort of soft
limestone, cemented by a material more resembling
mud than mortar. There is a comparative dearth of
woodland, and few fences — shepherds being largely
substituted for the latter. The grass is of a lighter
green than ours. The roads, though much better
than the American, are very inferior to the English.
Their vehicles, of whatever sort, are not so good as

ours. So of their horses, which are smaller. What hideous noises their drivers make! The dexterity with which these diligence horses are shifted is admirable, and might be taken as a specimen of Johnny Crapo's superiority in quickness of action to John Bull, and even to Brother Jonathan.

Arrived at Paris at 6 P.M. We stayed at the Hotel de Lille and Albion, at the entrance of Rue St. Thomas du Louvre, close to the Palais Royal, taking a comfortable room with two beds in it together.

From July 14 *to* 29. — A whirl of sixteen days' sight-seeing in this wonderful Paris and its environs! Yet one gets through with Paris sooner than with London, and a thousand-fold easier. The stranger, in the one, has every conceivable facility furnished him for visiting its multitudinous objects of interest; in the other, almost none at all. Museums, churches, palaces, hospitals, halls of legislation, temples of justice, colleges, galleries of pictures and statuary, royal manufactories, all are here gratuitously accessible, and foreigners are even especially favored; whereas, in England, one meets a hundred obstacles, some of them provoking and *expensive* enough in one's efforts to visit such places.

How can a sane man think of journalizing such a visit as this? What could one say of the Louvre, of the Musée de l'Histoire Naturelle au Jardin du Roi, of the Palace of Versailles, of the Bibliotheque du Roi, of that old charnel-house of monarchs at St. Denis, of even St. Cloud, Napoleon's favorite residence, or any one of a hundred other objects? I have visited these and many other objects of interest repeatedly. I will leave them for other travellers to describe. Père la Chaise disappointed me. It is less beautiful, exhibits less of good taste, than I had supposed. It seems to me greatly inferior to our Mount Auburn. The grounds are all ashes. Who loves to see a cemetery in an ash-heap, though it *be* stuck over with trees and covered with myriads of marble monuments? The practice of decorating the graves with flowers, which from their freshness must be often renewed, struck me as beautiful, though it may seem to say, "Our friends are *here*."

The anniversary of "The Three Days" occurred while I was there. It was the decade celebration of that revolution. All the other pageants I ever witnessed would, if combined in one, dwindle into insignificance, in respect of grandeur and numbers, in comparison of this. Some sixty thousand troops, richly uniformed, were in the procession, which probably included half a million of people, and with its magnificent "triumphal car" containing the remains of the victims of the three days, moved from the old church in rear of the Louvre through the Place de Louis XV. and the boulevards to the Place de la Bastille. It was flanked on both sides with such multitudes as could crowd themselves into the spacious sidewalks of the noble streets through which it passed, while the tops and windows of the numberless buildings in the vicinity were filled with spectators. There was some disappointment at the non-appearance in the procession of the king. He appeared at one of the windows of the Louvre, but I was too far from them to see him.

He has come to be chary of his person, in deference, it is said, to the wishes of his family, for nobody, I believe, doubts Louis Phillippe's personal courage. An incident occurred — I think it was in the Boulevard St. Martin — which must have made many feel that they were in the midst of another revolution. The crowds on either side of the procession at that point turned suddenly and attempted, though nearly in vain, to retreat; the soldiers had fixed their bayonets and quickened their movements. And such a mass of terror-stricken faces! The cause of this I did not learn until seeing it stated in the newspapers of the next morning. A company of tailors and others with revolutionary mottoes inscribed on its banners, commenced singing the Marseillaise Hymn, had made an attempt to join the procession, and was repulsed. That was all. But I had fancied for hours before this occurrence that I could see in a thousand faces an apprehension of another revolutionary outbreak. The French seem to me, like certain combustible materials, liable by the slightest spark to be kindled into a conflagration.

July 30. — Left Paris last evening, arriving in Boulogne early this afternoon. The road from Paris here was, I think, constructed as a military road. It must have been used when Napoleon assembled his legions at B. to attack England. We passed through several walled towns. The French seem particularly gregarious. In the agricultural districts, instead of living scattered, as with us, they congregate in several villages.

Having time, I wandered all over Boulogne, viewing its fortifications, &c. Walked far out of the place to the Napoleon Tower. A few days — I don't know but it was the very next day — afterwards, Louis Napoleon made his quixotic attack on the town. Were I endowed with prescience, I should have been tempted to await the onset.

Left in a steam packet for London.

London, August 2. — Went to Chelsea with Professor Adam. Alas! that extraordinary writer and steam-engine sort of thinker, Thomas Carlyle, had left here only a few hours before for a few days' "rustification" in the country. His pleasant, bright wife talked with us an hour or two, and made us laugh at her graphic description of her husband's outfit and departure, who, it seems, had left on an old Rosinante with saddlebags filled with maps of England, tobacco and pipes. She showed us a picture in oil of him. 'Twas only the head and a portion of the neck, having a remarkably healthful Scotch look and a massive forehead. Mrs. C. said he was much pleased with the Quaker lady, — Mrs Mott, — whose quiet manner had a soothing effect on him. She spoke of her husband's regard and respect for Ralph Waldo Emerson. I was *so* sorry not to find Carlyle at home. Had I not all along fancied I could easily see him, I should have made an earlier effort. Before his return, I shall probably have left London forever.

August 3. — Sat to Haydon at his studio, for the third and last time. The "revolutionary" look remains, heightened by the proximity of one of those placid Quakers. W. I. Fox, so well known to the American Unitarian public by his volumes of thrilling

sermons and other literary productions of great power and beauty, is one of the most remarkable men I
have met. I went to the Finsbury Square chapel
to hear him preach. He speaks as well as he writes,
and without notes; this is a rare coincidence of powers. His preaching is like O. A. Brownson's, it concerns the living. He grapples with questions that
come home to the businesses and hearts of men. It
were worth going a long way to hear such a man. His
object on this occasion was to enforce the practice of
honesty. The exposure he made of some of its popular infringements was striking. He attacked with
indignant severity the relation of lawyer and client
as defined by Lord Brougham, whose definition he
read to us. He rebuked the practice of using arguments one knows to be unsound for the sake of carrying one's point, and traced to this practice as their
source many inconsistencies which appear in authors,
in parliamentary speeches, in political and theological discussions. In this connection, he referred to a
speech of Lord John Russell's, and related an appropriate anecdote of some other parliamentary debater,
who had employed an argument which another knew
he believed to be unsound. " You had no confidence
in the soundness of that argument," said the other.
" Why did you employ such an argument? "—" I know
it, but then, how it told on the House ! " was the reply.
In the course of his sermon, — though some would
not call it a sermon, as it had no passage of scripture
tacked to its head, — Mr. Fox pronounced a brilliant
eulogy on Washington. The strong hold acquired
by that great man on the affections of his country-

men, and the admiration his name has inspired where-ever known, were attributed chiefly to his inflexible honesty.

After the audience had retired, I was introduced to him; and, a few days subsequently, called, by his invitation, at his residence, 13 Queen Square, Westminster, very near Dr. Bowring's, and had a long conversation with him. We talked of the popular preaching, of the Church establishment, of the voluntary system of popular education, of the ballot, and the unrighteous means resorted to by the rich and powerful to control the votes of the comparatively poor and feeble; of O'Connell and the repeal question. "You must vote so, or you shall have no more of my patronage, or you shall quit my employ." It is no uncommon thing in England, according to Dr. Fox, to hear such language as this addressed to a shopkeeper, a tenant, or one employed by him; and Mr. Fox inferred from our newspapers that the same evil prevailed, to some extent, in America. But I assured him this is not the case. Though partisan newspapers sometimes charged the practice on members of the opposite party, I doubted if an American, having any reputation to lose, would dare to be guilty of it. Mr. Fox is laboring to introduce the ballot in England as a means of delivering the people from this particular evil, and put sundry earnest questions to me relative to its working in our country. America was recently alluded to, he said, by a distinguished member in Parliament, to show that where the support of religion is left to the will of the people, it always fails of being adequately supported. I referred to *this* fact: that the city of Lowell, Mass., with a population of only some sixteen thousands, most of whom are operatives and women, has twelve or fifteen churches, many of them beautiful and most of them commodious, and ventured a strong doubt if in all Victoria's realm there could be found such an example of liberality in the support of religious institutions.

I am informed by Dr. Southward Smith that Mr. Fox's audience is composed of an intellectual, thinking class of persons. In person he is very short and fleshy. The most striking features of his physiognomy are his eyes, which are black and piercing. He has a rich and powerful voice.

My channel of introduction to Dr. Southward Smith was Dr. Bowring. The latter is an LL.D., the former an M.D. One short interview only have I had with him, though I have twice been invited to dine with him. I have called several times on him, as he has on me and I was unfortunately out. That interview, should I have no other, as I hope to have before my return, I shall prize highly, since, if it has not otherwise benefited me, it gratified a strong desire I had long felt to see the author of "Illustrations of the Divine Government." I mentioned to Dr. Smith that the American edition of that work was published at my recommendation. It is remarkable that the same individual should have written so ably on subjects so different — I refer to his work on Fever — as theology and medicine. He spoke of Livingston's "Criminal Code" in terms of very high approbation.

The American delegation owe many thanks to Samuel Gurney for the fine entertainment given on their account by him to-day at his princely residence at Upton, West Ham, near Stratford. Mr. Gurney is a brother to Joseph John Gurney and to Mrs. Frye, and a brother-in-law to Thomas Fowell Buxton, who was one of the party. He is a wealthy banker, and a member of the society of Friends. This magnificent place, with its beautiful parks and gardens, once the property and the abode of the famous Dr. Fothergill, came into Mr. Gurney's possession by his wife.

The Duchess of Sutherland, her daughter — a lovely girl with a fine head — and Lord Morpeth, secretary for Ireland, honored the party with their presence. The Duchess holds the highest office filled by any woman under the crown, that of Mistress of the Robes. She is said to be the most beautiful woman in the country. She has quite convinced me of the reality of those forms which I have been wont to regard as the creations of poets, painters and sculptors. Her features, judged by the American standard, are above the average size; so also is her person. Her hair is light brown, and her eyes are blue. The Duchess is not less distinguished for the splendid parties she gives than for her personal charms. The mere lighting of her palace on one of these occasions, I am told, costs five thousand dollars. She is a great lover and patron of the fine arts, and has honored Garrison, and herself still more, by requesting him to sit to Haydon for his portrait. These noble persons all appeared to do their best to make themselves agreeable to the party. I enjoyed this visit greatly. The weather, the drive, — seven miles out of London, — our host, his daughters and the company, were delightful; so were the hedges, the gardens, the green lawns, the winding walks and the deer. Our host sent some dozen carriages to take us out to his place and back to the city.

Took tea at Dr. Beattie's at 6 Park Square, Regent's Park, a most lovely part of the city. Dr. Madden — to whose intimacy with Beattie I was indebted for this visit — had led me to expect that Carlyle, Dickens and Bulwer might be there, but neither came. The doctor is as sociable and pleasant as he is literary and gifted. He is of Scotch origin, and a relative of the author of the famous "Essay on Truth." His family, he told me, were despoiled of their property for political offences, or for religious ones. He is the author of beautifully illustrated histories of Scotland, Switzerland, &c. He was physician to William IV., and continues a special favorite of the Queen Dowager, Adelaide, who commanded a handsome medal to be struck, as an expression of regard for him. The doctor's wife showed me a pair of cuffs knit by the Queen, and presented to him once when they were travelling together on the continent.

Took tea for the second time at Mrs. Reed's, 6 Grenville Street, Brunswick Square. She is a widow "of substance," and a Unitarian, having one of her rooms adorned with busts of our Dr. Channing and of other clergymen.

Lady Byron was of the party. She was at several of our convention meetings, but I was not introduced to her till now. She is interested especially in Abolition, as every one having a heart must needs be. I could not do less than tender to Lady Byron my heartfelt thanks for the service she had rendered and was rendering to our great cause. There are thousands of boasting republicans in America who, though deaf to the voice of reason, justice, humanity, be it uttered in tones of thunder even, will yet be moved by the example and conduct of Britons high in rank, wealth and fashion. So I told her ladyship. I explained to her the causes which keep, with us, so many of "the better sort" aloof from the Abolition movement. Our conversation closed with the interchange of a few words touching her son-in-law, the Earl of Lovelace. This interview with Lady Byron did much to remove the prejudice I had entertained against her. My sympathies had been with Byron in the unfortunate matter of their separation. Her ladyship seems as amiable as she is certainly a benevolent and intellectual woman. She has established a charity-school. It has some hundreds of pupils, who are supported entirely by herself. They appear to be much attached to their benefactress, I am told by Mrs. Mott, who visited the school. Lady Byron travelled on the continent for the purpose of acquainting herself with the most approved modes of education, preparatory to establishing her school. In religion she is no sectarian, but favors the Unitarians. I have been told her son-in-law is the only nobleman in the kingdom known to have attended a Unitarian church. I remember Lord Byron, in his conversation with Dr. Kennedy, who attempted to convert his lordship to the dogmas of the church, speaks of Lady Byron as being "a great gun among the Unitarians."

Dr. Hutton, who was present, is the principal Unitarian clergyman of the British metropolis. He is past the meridian of life. How "clever" he is I have little means of judging. I like him for having permitted Mrs. Mott to hold a religious meeting in his chapel. We talked of the difficulties connected with the question of slavery in our country. I cannot learn that the English Unitarians, as a body, have taken much interest in the Abolition movement. It is a sorry comment on the "liberality" of the sect. Some excuse, however, may be found for them in the great prejudice existing against them in other sects, which would naturally hinder all co-operation of others in behalf of a cause to which all might be equally friendly.

Mrs. Opie is known to almost all Americans by her work on "Lying," as well as by several others. I wished to-night that I knew more of her writings, of which, in truth, I know almost nothing; for I spent the evening at her house, and it would of course have been pleasant to be able to talk with her of her works. She has written some tales of an anti-slavery character. She is an exceedingly agreeable woman, and, as an author, is uncommonly modest. She took special pains to "draw me out," or, at least, to make my visit a very happy one. She has a fine gallery of pictures, which I enjoyed much.

Took tea at Mr. II. Spark's, a Quaker banker, who once swallowed a forged note on the witness-stand to save the criminal from conviction, and consequent death.

To-day I dined with Mr. Turnbull, to whom I was introduced by Dr. Madden. My impressions of him are most favorable. He is a Scotchman by birth, has spent some time in Cuba as an agent of the government, and has a plan of his own for abolishing the slave trade. His plan is developed in his late work, a good-sized octavo. He is a man of undoubted talents, and, like many another talented man, is unable to do himself any justice in speaking in public. He introduced me to Miss Americus Vespucius, the only living descendant of the alleged discoverer of America. She returned not long since from a visit to America, where an effort was made to obtain for her a national donation as an expression of regard for her illustrious ancestor. That effort having failed, numbers of "patriotic" individuals made her the offer of a handsome pecuniary present, which, however, she declined to accept, thinking it might have been proposed under an impression that she needed assistance. A more captivating woman I have never met. There is a witchery about her that is irresistible, that even Zeno himself could hardly have withstood the influence of. The Duchess of Sutherland struck me as being as elegant and perhaps the most beautiful woman I had ever seen ; but those are not the epithets applicable to Vespucius. She is exquisitely pretty and fascinating. The Italian is much the younger, apparently, has a more delicate, slender form, sylph-like indeed, more grace and sprightliness, a dark complexion, a profusion of black hair, and very large flashing eyes, whose beauty is heightened by their long silken lashes. But what is better, her mental qualities are of a superior order. She has great conversational powers and speaks several different languages. And with all these charms of person and superiority of intellect, she is said to possess another quality, not frequently found in the fairer part of creation. It is an Amazonian courage, of which Dr. Madden told me she once gave a singular proof, by pistolling a Frenchman who had dared to insult her. She has been for some time an exile from her native Florence on account of her political opinions. I met her again after this at the soirée, where that animated countenance and those speaking eyes appeared to evince as deep an interest in the proceedings as was felt by those who might be thought to understand them better.

Newcastle, August 9. — Arrived here to-day. It being Sunday I went to the Unitarian Church, and was introduced to the sister of Miss Martineau, Mrs. Greenhow, whose husband is a successful medical practitioner. Dined with them at their place, 28 Eldon Square, and afterwards made a delightful visit to their sister Harriet, at Tynemouth, where she is now passing her time in a quiet little cottage, sufficiently near Dr. Greenhow to have the benefit of his medical skill, for she has been long an invalid, and indeed is without all hope of recovery. Did ever woman talk so like a book? Oh, it *was* a rich treat the two or three hours I passed with her! She thinks the use of her *large* ear-trumpet has *improved* her hearing. One finds it as easy conversing with her as with one not deaf.

August 10, *Melrose, Abbotsford.* — Arrived at the first of these places last evening. Sauntered a long time among the favorite ruins of Sir Walter Scott, or — to correct the Hibernicism — of Melrose Abbey, one of Sir Walter's favorite haunts. Couldn't "see them by moonlight," because of a drizzly rain.

The eastern window Scott thus describes :

> "The moon on the east oriel shone,
> Through slender shafts of shapely stone,
> By foliaged tracery combined ;
> Thou wouldst have tho't some fairy hand
> 'Twixt poplars straight the osier wand,
> In many a freakish knot had twined ;
> Then framed a spell when the work was done,
> And changed the willow wreath to stone."

11. — At 6 in the morning I walked to Abbotsford, "solitary and alone," not doubting but I should find out when I reached it. Soon casting a "glower" down on some of its turrets through an opening, I found myself right upon this most unique structure of gray and red sandstone, fancifully arranged, and speedily descending the hill entered the gate, and had at once a full view of its front with my back to the silvery Tweed. An old woman, issuing from the lodge, conducted me through the most interesting apartments of this home of the mighty "Wizard of the North." To me there was the greatest interest in his library or study, whence issued those wonderful fictions that have astonished and enraptured the world. I sat down in his comfortable arm-chair at

his convenient writing-desk, and, as Orville Dewey
says of himself on a similar occasion, "it was enough."
In a small side-closet, with a glass door, is the suit
of clothes in which Scott last went forth to look on
those beautiful grounds, a goodly portion of whose
numerous trees were planted by his own hand. It is
painful to think to what toil he was finally pushed by
that almost insane love of acres and a palace to which
this singular Abbotsford owes its origin. What sig-
nifies it all now? Were the present Sir Walter Scott
"a chip of the old block," the toil and anxiety of the
elder had not seemed quite so utterly wasted. He
has gone to India. I have heard it said he has been
known to boast of not having read his father's tales.
However, it is not improbable that Scott would rather
his son were a warrior, in possession of a palace and
the usual trappings of nobility, though a fool, than
such another as himself, without these appendages.
I have a hundred-fold more reverence for Burns than
I could ever feel for Scott. The former's "a man's
a man for a' that," must have seemed the veriest nonsense to the latter. The head of a fine portrait of
him I saw here is considerably lower than in the casts
I have been accustomed to see of Sir Walter. His
wife, whose picture hangs beside her husband's, must
have been beautiful. I rode to the great magician's
last resting-place at Dryburgh. The scenery about
here is greatly exaggerated in the descriptions I have
read. I was half disposed to fling my guide-book
away, of vexatious disappointment at its bombastic
descriptions. The hills that loom up so in the draw-
ings, and the Tweed, that seems so noble a river, —

why, a man of my longitudinal developments might
almost bestride the one, as, without wetting his hips,
he certainly could ford the other.   The Eildon Hills
— there is a trinity of them — should be excepted
from this remark.   They seemed almost equally near,
in my rambles, whether I was at the distance of one
mile or several, — a proof that they are considerable
hills.

August 11, *Edinburgh.* — I enjoyed the ride
hither by coach, from Melrose, much.   Taking it all
in all, the New Town, with its airy regular streets,
its spacious, comfortable and often elegant dwellings,
the adjacent scenery of land and water, of ocean and
friths, of mountains and lawns, is the delightfulest
city I have yet found.

George Combe, his brother, Dr. Andrew Combe,
George Thompson and John Dunlop have been very
kind and attentive to me.   Dunlop accompanied me
to see the Parliament House, its courts of law, the
Palace of Holyrood, the castle, &c.   The lawyers,
judges, philosophers and literati of this "Athens" of
the British kingdom are now pretty much absent, it
being a season of general vacation.   At Holyrood the
chief object of interest was Mary's bed-chamber, very
much as that unfortunate victim of Elizabeth left it.
"The virgin Queen!"   "Good Queen Bess!"   Is it
not marvellous that English authors should prate thus
of that old termagant?   Notwithstanding her ability,
which, like that of Beelzebub, certainly deserves
respect, I have nowhere seen her stiff, starched image,
so often met with in these realms, no incident has
called her to mind but I have experienced a feeling

of abhorrence and disgust. I would rather a thousand-fold have been the murdered Mary.

George Combe, with his wife, is living a little out of the city in a beautiful cottage. I spent a good portion of the 13th there, dining with him and taking a drive. He thinks Horace Mann the greatest man he met in America and doing the most for his country by his efforts in behalf of education. Grave as Combe is, he can be satirical. I was amused to hear him speak of the popular theology and doctors of divinity of the day, saying of the latter, in that deep guttural tone and Scottish accent of his, "I would like to see one of them just put into the pit they tell so much of and kept there about a fortnight, and see what he would think of it." Mrs. Combe is a daughter of Mrs. Siddons, of whom she showed me a picture. That celebrated actress must have been as beautiful as gifted, judging by this finely executed portrait. In the evening we took tea at the residence of his brother Andrew, "physician to the Queen in Scotland," who, considering his great attainments in science, literature and philosophy, is almost painfully diffident in his manners — the reverse of George. He is a bachelor, and from a principle which, as the world now is, indicates a nice sense of justice or a strong feeling of benevolence, or both. He has a constitutional tendency to consumption. That is the cause of his abstinence from marriage.

This was a day to be remembered. What is all your sight-seeing, your gazing on castles, palaces, temples, and even nature's magnificent scenery, in comparison of converse with men and women?

I dined with John Dunlop, who keeps a bachelor's hall at Randolph Cliff. He has travelled in America. He took pains to obtain a picture, in oil, of Daniel Webster which, on account of some late manifestation of the "Godlike's" pro-slaveryism, he now keeps face to the wall.

Breakfasted with George Thompson and his wife yesterday, and their son born in America. He is a feeble child, owing, doubtless, to the perpetual alarm and excitement of Mrs. Thompson caused by the mobocratic assaults on her husband.

I visited an assembly of three hundred divines, more or fewer, now in town, where the matter "was up" of the Church's independence. I asked Dunlop to let me try if I could identify Dr. Chalmers in this great crowd of parsons. I succeeded, and by my phrenology alone; for apart from the reverend doctor's cerebral configuration there was nothing peculiar in his person corresponding to any preconception of mine. He has the look of a brawny yeoman. I heard him speak at some length in the debate, or tried to, rather, for I was at too great a distance to understand much that he said, and probably was but poorly compensated by reading a report of his speech in the morning papers. His manner was earnest and ungainly. He held his cane in one hand, clutching it near midway and cutting the air with it, in outrageous violation of Hamlet's advice, the perspiration standing in big drops on that noble forehead and embrowned face. George Combe has modified my opinion of the merits of this church battle, and quite destroyed the sympathy I had felt for these clerical warriors against secular influence with the rights of churches, by showing that the special object of their hostility is, under the circumstances, favorable to the growth of religious liberality.

August 15. — Left Edinburgh yesterday by coach, to go on a steamer on the Firth of Forth. 'Twas a little after nightfall when I reached Callander. Rose at 4.30, taking breakfast at 5, this morning, and by 5.30 was footing it to the nearest shore of Loch Katrine, some ten miles distant, which I hoped to reach in season for the boat, which, by some strange misapprehension, I had supposed to be a small steamer. The result of this supposition was the necessity of walking an additional fifteen miles. Yet, so exquisite and exhilarating is the scenery of all this route, my twenty-five miles of walking caused me very little fatigue. Some of the pleasantest views I caught in this pedestrian tour were those of the mountains, among which were Ben Ledi, Ben Venue and Ben Voirlich, with Ben Lomond, more than 3000 feet high, towering above them all. Their tops were covered with mist, which, by the action of wind and sun, aided by my own perpetually changing position, imparted to the mountains a thousand ever-varying forms and all the variegated coloring of the rainbow. And such seemed the profusion and wild *confusion* of those mountains, one might easily fancy they marked the place in which the Titans of old met and flung such things at each other. By Cousin's theory of the influence of external nature on character, the Highlanders should be among the most poetic of the races.

Took the steamer for Glasgow, arriving in this

splendid business city at about sunset, never before in any single day having seen so much to gratify my love of the beautiful.

Visited the Normal School here. Was delighted with what I saw of the process of training children. If all children, thought I, were so trained, how irresistibly attractive would be many a school now so repulsive ! Physical exercise and amusement are not less attended to than what usually passes for education. Such unrestrained familiarity between teachers and pupils would, in the schools which it was my misfortune to be flung into when a boy, have been deemed tantamount to an abandonment of all order and discipline, to misrule and anarchy. The instruction is chiefly communicated orally. The word "cough" having been used, a class of little fellows showed not only that they understood its orthography and meaning, but also that the cause or causes of the thing meant were understood by them, evincing, indeed, a familiarity with the structure and functions of the human body, and the influence on these of heat and cold, of dryness and moisture, &c., which would be creditable to some in our country who professedly practice "the healing art."

August 18 *and* 19. — Made a *pilgrimage* — for it was nothing else — to the birthplace of the immortal Burns, of which, since I cannot speak of it as I would, I almost hesitate to speak at all. I don't know but it is the only pilgrimage I ever made, unless I may so designate my visit to Stratford-upon-Avon. Nor was I moved to it by my admiration of Robert Burns as a poet, albeit he towers above all other

Scottish bards farther than his favorite Ben Lomond rises above the hills that surround it. It was by my reverence for him as a man, and sympathy with his sorrows. To my vision, the splendors of his poesy, brilliant as these are, pale before the glories of such a manhood. It needs no effort to prove that Burns was neither a sot nor a rake.

It was near sundown when I reached "Old Ayr." I hastened to find the poet's birthplace, distant three miles from the city, in the hope of finding lodgings under the same roof, of which, alas! I was disappointed. "Johnny Goodie" and Mrs. Johnny Goodie were in bed when I got there, and no entreaties of mine could prevail on them to let me in. I therefore had to return to the city for lodgings, almost vexed by my disappointment, yet pleased to have made the attempt, since my six miles' walk over ground so often pressed by the feet of Burns could hardly be otherwise than pleasurable. The next morning, before sunrise, I was mounted in a gig, and on my way to the "banks and braes o' bonnie Doon," crossing "the Auld Brig" and "the New Brig," and bethinking me just here of the sad catastrophe that chanced to "Tam O'Shanter's Mare." I had no guide with me, and felt the need of none, so easily could I distinguish the principal objects of interest by recollection of the poet's descriptions. The walls of "Kirk Alloway" remain, and I entered within them. In its little graveyard I noticed the humble slab of Burns' honored father, a stern yet tender parent, with good sense enough to supply a small democracy, and honesty enough to suffice for a dozen, as "democratic institu-

tions" usually go.   Saw the interior of the monu-
mental temple.   It contains a picture in oil, below
the natural size of the poet — a copy from the original
by Naysmith.   "Johnny Goodie" showed me a little
indentation on the wall where lay the cot on which
Burns was born.   "Johnny" must have been among
the poet's "drouthy neeburs," for he assured me he
had "drunk many a glass of whiskey with Rob."
He is very old.   I found it difficult to understand
him, his Scottish accent is so strong.

The scenery hereabouts, I suspect, looks now very
much as when the bard lived and sang in its midst.
It is not remarkable for beauty in such a country as
"Auld Scotia."   Returned to Glasgow on the 19th.

The Scotch are an earnest people, as every people
believing in a veritable God must needs be.   There
is therefore a remarkable absence of cant among
them.   I do not suppose Robert Burns would be
taken as a model of saintliness by them.   But I find
enough in him of manly piety to set up quite a denomination of Christians in some quarters.   I know
that Burns, like Scott, sometimes swore.   But who
can say there may not have been as little of profanity
in the swearing of either, as there is of piety in the
praying of men who have anathematized both?

Of the characteristics of Scottish literature, I know
not what an appreciative observer might say.   But
I am quite sure all will agree with me that the Scotch
have contributed their full share to wellnigh every
department of literature, using the word in its largest
sense.   In that of history, they may well be proud of
having produced such names as those of Robertson,

Hume and Mackintosh. In philosophy and criticism, Adam Smith, Beattie, Kane, Reid, Stewart, Brown, Blair, George Campbell, Brougham, Jeffrey, Welch, Chalmers and Carlyle are names which no nation need be ashamed of. In mathematical and physical science, they may well exult in having given to the world the Gregorys, Hutton, Black, Playfair and Brewster. In practical science, the name of Watts alone were sufficient to elicit the highest admiration of all who can appreciate the literature of the steam engine. And in poetry and fiction, they must be a paltry people who would not throw their caps sky-high in honor of such men as Barbour, Ramsay, Thomson, Burns, Cunningham, Hogg and Thomas Campbell, Smollett, Mackenzie, Armstrong, Scott, Galt and Wilson. In law, too, and medicine and divinity, — callings all of them which must needs be plied so long as men shall continue to violate the higher laws of their physical, moral and religious constitution, — the Scotch have furnished an array of names united to dignify and adorn that whole trinity of " the learned professions."

Arrived at Belfast, Ireland, on the 20th. I met on board the steamer yesterday Mr. George H. Girle, merchant, of Edinburgh. He is a Unitarian, and is an especial admirer of W. J. Fox. He has ridden several miles out with me to introduce me to Rev. Dr. Montgomery, who stands the highest in his shoes, and fills the widest space, of all the parsons I have met, even on this side of the water — a sort of Jeremiah Mason physically, and even something more intellectually — yet not clumsy of person, but

a handsome man withal. He has for some time filled
a professional chair in the college here, though not
without a strong, and I believe somewhat violent,
opposition, excited by his Unitarianism. The Unitarians in Ireland all claim to be Presbyterians — a
claim which gives them certain advantages, both
pecuniary and otherwise. He wished me to spend
the day with him in his pretty abode. And how I
wished I might!

Dublin, August 21. — Arrived at this beautiful
capital of Old Ireland a little after nightfall. On
alighting from the coach was suddenly laid hands on
by Richard D. Webb, who was in waiting for me.
This *was* pleasant.

August 22. — James Haughton and O'Connell called
this morning. Breakfasted with the former at his
house, and then spent an hour with the latter at his
home in Merrion Square. O'Connell talked chiefly
of "the Repeal," of the danger of war with France,
which latter he pronounced inevitable unless England
should basely knuckle. Several of his grandchildren
were running in and out, receiving the great agitator's caresses, who occasionally dandled one on his
knee. He promised the Irish, at the Corn Exchange
the other morning, twenty years more of service,
saying his family had a trick of living till they were
upwards of eighty. I think he told me his grandmother had twenty-three children, all of whom lived
beyond that age. Dr. Madden told me that he is
himself one of a family of twenty-five children. Richard Allen's father has ten living, and has lost five.
Dined with this fine old gentleman. The ten children

were all present. It is a country residence, six or
eight miles out of the city, called "Mountain View."
Quite a company at dinner. The older ones took
wine, I noticed. Richard, — the son, — R. D. Webb
and James Haughton are teetotallers — a sort of
temperance trinity in Dublin.

George P. Downes, distinguished by his literary
and antiquarian pursuits, and connected with the University here, a philanthropist, moreover, though of
too feeble health and mild a temperament, were he
less absorbed by the pursuits just named, to plunge
into the stormy arena of Reform, accompanied me to
St. Patrick's Cathedral. Listened to the music awhile
— looked at the monuments to Dean Swift and
Stella. Walked in St. Stephen's Green, the largest
in Europe. Should not suppose Wellington's Pyra-
mid could have cost so much — £20,000. Tea at
Richard Allen's. Breakfast yesterday at "Green-
mount," a delightful place, at Richard D. Webb's
father's. The old gentleman is one of those comfortable Quakers who understand so well how to
secure the good things of "this present world" while
seeking those of the next.

FATHER MATTHEW.

So anxious was I to see and hear this Apostle of
Temperance, that I relinquished for that purpose the
pleasure of visiting the Lakes of Killarney, so remarkable for the richness and beauty of their scenery.
It was a sacrifice by no means inconsiderable. It
was one, however, which I do not regret to have
made; for the pleasure I derived from hearing him

address a multitude of his countrymen on the advantages of teetotalism, from seeing him perform the touching ceremony of administering the pledge to many hundreds of them, and especially from my personal interviews with the great cold-water reformer, was a pleasure which, even if I were a poet, I would not willingly have foregone for glimpses of all the lake and mountain scenery in which Ireland so richly abounds. I went the first time to hear him speak, in a romantic and lovely place, half a dozen miles from the city. A prettier place for addressing such a multitude — the papers next morning stated the number present to be twenty thousand — could hardly be wished. A platform was erected for the occasion on the margin of a spacious lawn, whose opposite extremity was skirted by a range of beautiful hills. As Father Matthew worked his way slowly through the dense crowd, all classes manifested the greatest eagerness to catch his eye and draw from him some token of recognition, and threw themselves in his path to receive on their bended knees the good man's blessing, which was cheerfully bestowed in all practicable instances. These genuflexions affected me unpleasantly until I reflected that the persons performing them were Catholics, and that this was one of their modes of manifesting the religious sentiment, whose manifestations, under whatever form, ought always to command our respect. The speech was a plain, straightforward, matter-of-fact statement of the evils of drunkenness and the blessings of temperance, by which was meant abstinence from *all* that intoxicates; of the selfishness and folly of all

who oppose the great reform — uttered with the earnestness of an honest man, conscious of the importance of his cause, and therefore carrying conviction
to the minds of "such as should be saved." I was
delighted to hear him say that nearly three millions
had taken the pledge, and departures from its principles had been rare. The pledge is so framed that
any one may be released from its obligations by sig-
nifying to Father Matthew his wish to be released.
Ireland's greatest calamity, he said, was the intemperance of her sons. There was no need of emigra-
tion to better their fortunes. He had, within the last
week, passed over millions of acres of the richest soil,
into which the spade had never been put. Let them
be teetotallers, and they could get on at home. If
they were drunkards, they could get on well nowhere. Be, then, he continued, teetotallers, and you
have everything to hope and nothing to fear. Of
crime you will not be suspected, for all know that it
is alcohol alone that makes the Irishman a criminal.
If a bailiff enter your cabin in pursuit of a criminal,
tell him you are a teetotaller, and he will at once infer he is on the wrong track, and make off. Be teetotallers, and you will be blessed with health, with
happy wives and children, enough to eat, to drink,
and to wear, and, dying, "you may be buried like
princes." This last consideration were a small mo-
tive to an American; but to an Irishman it has a
potency that can scarce be overestimated. Often,
nothing, except his soul's safety, is more coveted by
the latter than the honors of a "decent funeral."
After closing his speech, in which allusion was made

to the presence of an American teetotaller, by his
request I addressed the multitude.   Father Matthew
is not an eloquent man, and there is nothing striking
in his personal appearance, excepting an expression
of great benevolence in his countenance.   I took
breakfast with him the next morning, when we talked
of temperance, tithes, Catholicism, the clergy, *et
cetera*.

I called on Richard Carmichael to-day — the biog-
rapher and friend of Spurzheim, to whom I brought
a letter of introduction from George Combe.   He
presented me a copy of " Theology and Metaphysics,"
in two stout octavos.

This Dublin is the quietest city I ever saw, considering its magnitude.

Capt. Basil Hall, in his "Fragments of Voyages
and Travels," says truly, " It is far easier to get into
a house in Ireland than to get out of it again, for
there is an attractive witchery about the hospitality
of the natives which has no match, so far as I have
seen, anywhere else in the wide world.   In other
places the people are hospitable and kind to a stranger
as the case may be, but here it is reduced to a science ;
a web of attentions is flung round the visitor before he
well knows where he is.   So that if he be not very
cold-blooded, or very clear-sighted, or a very tem-
perate man, it will cost him sundry headaches — and
mayhap some touches of the *heart*ache — before he
wins his way back to his former tranquility."

August 31. — James Haughton and his two young-
est daughters, R. D. Webb, his wife and myself,
made an excursion to the Wicklow Mountains, having

a picnic at the foot of the beatiful Dargle, and in returning a run on the shores of Lough Bray. What a social time we had of it! How I romped with those pretty girls! How we sprinkled one another with that pure water from the Dargle, and how their father and I waked the echoes of Lough Bray's surrounding hills as we shouted! And what laughable Irish stories Richard told to us, good as any in the book! Richard's house has been my headquarters ever since I came here. All the Irish friends here have been so kind and attentive that it is painful to leave them. But I must go to-morrow.

Liverpool, September 3. — Arrived here to-day by steamer, having left Dublin — or Queenstown — the previous afternoon. Richard Webb and Richard Allen accompanied me to Queenstown. Heaven bless them and theirs, and all the dear Irish friends!

Joseph Pease and his daughter Elizabeth called on me early, telling me George Thompson would soon arrive from Manchester to see me off. Mr. Thompson did not disappoint the expectation they excited. He arrived this afternoon, and we have been rambling every whither, and talking of a hundred and one things. He pointed out to me the place in which he held the discussion with Bosthwick. We went to see the picture of the "Temptation." After this rode some miles out of the city, to call at Mr. Wilson's, where Mr. Pease and his daughter are stopping.

Mr. Pease, his daughter and Mr. Thompson urged me to give over leaving on the "Britannia," remain a few months longer and accompany the last in a lecturing tour, to stir up the people in behalf of India, as "the remedy for slavery the world over." Mr. Pease even offered to remove one objection that I had paid my fare to America. I confess it was with great difficulty I could refuse compliance. Returned to the city, and sat up talking with Thompson till "high twelve" or past.

Came on board the "Britannia" this morning. Was delighted to see dear Thompson once more, who came on board in the "tug" which brought the mailbags, almost like a spirit of the air, so unexpected was his appearance.

At 2.30 we got under way, and I bade farewell to

> "This sceptered isle,
> This earth of Majesty, this seat of Mars,
> This other Eden, demi-paradise;
> This fortress, built by Nature for herself,
> Against infection and the hand of war;
> This happy breed of men, this little world;
> This precious stone set in the silver sea,
> Which serves it in the office of a wall,
> Or as a moat defensive to a house,
> Against the envy of less happier lands,
> This blessed spot, this earth, this realm, this England,
> .   .   .   .
> This land of such dear souls, this dear, dear land."

September 5. — Passed Cork, on which I cast "lingering, longing looks," wishing I could put my foot on its soil.

Sunday, 6. — The captain called at my stateroom before I was up, and invited me to preach. Know not how he knew I *could* preach. Declined the invitation, which was then extended to and accepted by a Methodist clergyman, who, I noticed on finishing his sermon, refreshed himself with a plentiful "horn" of wine. This gentleman said to me, "If the Methodists in England had known you were a relative of Rev. Samuel Bradburn, they would have carried you through the whole kingdom on their shoulders."

September 10. — There were several slaveholders' on board, and to-day we had a long and an earnest discussion of slavery, which excited a very general interest. At one point, a slaveholder said something personally threatening to myself. My response to this was as severe and indignant a rebuke as my knowledge of the Queen's English would enable me to make. He had forgotten that we were in the saloon of a British steamship, where, though trampled on with cowardly baseness in America, the right of free speech was likely to find protection. It was a luxury to meet such fellows in such a place. He said he would give me five thousand dollars if I would preach such doctrines in South Carolina; that he wished I would come there and try it; which gave me a fresh occasion of pouring contempt on the character he had thus avowed for himself and his brother-slaveholders. A little consequential French Count belonging to the suite of Lord Falkland, the newly appointed Governor of Nova Scotia, now on his way to assume that office, said, "If I owned slaves and you tell me I must give up de negroes, give up my property without compensation, I would say, away with you to de debil." Some hours after the discussion, the captain said to me, "You are the oddest man I ever knew. Why, I never saw one who had such a perfect command of himself, such an entire control of his feelings in a stormy debate, as you exhibited to-day." "I wish you would say that to some of my constituents, who believe me a real Hotspur, though you probably could not, without raising doubts of either your veracity or your sanity." But I think I *can* repress all manifestation of feeling and seem cool enough, when satisfied it is best to do so.

September 13. — To-day, had an opportunity rarely seen, to witness an encounter before breakfast, about the steamer's prow, of a whale, a thresher and a swordfish. The first was between the two latter; the thresher being on the back, and the swordfish under the belly of the leviathan ; the one keeping him down and the other up, the poor whale bellowing the while like a herd of Bashan's bulls. What was this, intelligence or instinct?

September 16. — Arrived at Halifax at 7 A.M., remaining till 11.30. Lord Falkland landed under an escort, and proceeded with some parade to the government house. I stopped not to witness the pageant, but busied myself with seeing as much as possible of this old town, which has a Nantucket aspect. It is a glorious, beautiful harbor.

September 17. — Cunard, who is a fellow-passenger from Halifax to Boston, showed a deal of surprise at my declining to take wine with him at dinner to-day, and asked if I had crossed the Atlantic without drinking any. I trust it may induce Mr. Cunard to consider the injustice of the practice, in his ships, of compelling persons who use no wine to pay for the wine of others. This abstinence has been one of the severest trials to which my alimentativeness was ever subjected; for the water we have used has been bad, and the milk worse, while the wines furnished have been pronounced excellent, and I have practised this self-denial not on my own account. ' Of some eighty cabin passengers I have been the only teetotaller on board.

September 18. — Arrived at East Boston.

The letter complimentary to the " Britannia " got up by the passengers before our arrival, I declined signing, because deeming its compliments undeserved so far as related to the fare, which was very inferior to that of the "Roscoe." I would willingly have joined in any praise of the captain.

Took breakfast at the Marlboro' House.

CHAPTER VI.

THE DOEFACE: EXTRACTS FROM A SPEECH AT A POLITICAL MEETING IN OHIO.

BUT for this prostitution of the national government to the support of slavery, the North, not the South, is mainly responsible. For the South has acted efficiently in that direction only by using the baser sort of Northern demagogues, into whose villanous foreheads John Randolph, the intensest hater of all meanness, many years ago burnt an infamous cognomen, which, like the mark of infamy that God set upon Cain, will last forever. The caustic Virginian, in his congressional seat, branded them as "*Doefaces.*" I am not sure but we have dulled the point of that pungent epithet by changing its original orthography. Randolph spelled the word, D-O-E-face, in allusion to the timid, startled looks of that animal, which is said to shrink from the reflection of its own face in the water.

May I ask your attention, for a few moments, to some observations on the natural history of this unique species of animal? We will glance, then, at some of his anatomical and physiological idiosyncracies. Perchance the glimpse may suggest, especially to those accustomed to mix something of the religious sentiment with their causal speculations, the final cause or the reason of the providential existence of so strange a biped. I am not myself sufficiently conversant with zoology to be able to say positively to what genus of the animated kingdom the Doughface belongs. From his general configuration, his mere outward form and seeming, a superficial observer might class him with some lower species of the genus *homo*. But this, if naturalists are right in excluding from that genus all invertebrated animals, would be to commit a grave error. For in every Doeface which I have had occasion to dissect, — and my scalpel, such as it is, has been employed on a considerable number of the species, — I have noticed an utter absence of the vertebral column popularly called the backbone. And I have observed the place of that column to be uniformly supplied by an elastic, cartilaginous substance, having apparently not the remotest tendency to ossification. There is likewise a structural peculiarity in the Doeface's knees, those articulations having a suppleness quite equalling the flexibility of his spinal cartilage.

His liver is of the lily complexion. His heart, — I beg pardon, gentlemen, for the Doeface *has* no heart. He is as destitute of that viscus as of a backbone.

That portion of the thoracic cavity which in other bipeds contains a heart, is in the Doughface occupied by only a muscle, formed merely to stir his diluted blood. He is remarkable, too, for the shape of his sconce; which, by the way, is perhaps the only osseous or bony formation beneath his whole epidermis. In different individuals of the tribe, the magnitude of that osseous structure varies. In some, it is as large as the head of a moderately intellectual man,

but in many, it is scarce bigger than a decent-sized
turnip, and its surface is diversified by miniature hills
and hollows, as if symbolizing its owner's "up sand
downs of life," if indeed it is proper to have used an
expression implying that the Doughface *owns* even
the head he carries.   But whatever differences of
both may obtain in the crania of Doughfaces, those
bony globes will all be found to present a striking
similarity of conformation at the superfices of certain
phrenological regions.

In those to which the ingenious philosophy of Gall
and Spurzheim assigns the cerebral organs of benevolence, veneration, conscientiousness, firmness and
self-esteem the cranium is very palpably depressed;
while in those of the organs of cautiousness, cunning
and the love of gain, it is strikingly protuberant.
The visual apparatus of the Doughface is also irregu-
larly organized.

Most of the species are mole-eyed. That is to say,
while clearly discerning objects lying about their
noses, they are blind as midday bats to all such as lie
a little remote from those nasal projections. And
there is a defect in the muscular fibres which control
the action of the Doughface's eyes. So that those
orbs, incapable of sustaining a straightforward look,
that is, of looking a man, especially an honest man,
steadily in the face, have a sidelong, furtive inclina-
tion such as you have seen in the optic organs of a
shabby dog returning from the commission of an act
for which it expected to be kicked. A reference
to only one other organic idiosyncrasy of the Doughface must close the anatomical part of this demonstra-

tion. I allude to the integument in which rests his corporeity. The human skin is so thickly interwoven with minute nerves of sensation that you cannot touch it with a pin's point without pricking some one or more of those nervous filaments, and so exciting the subject's sensibility. But it remains to be ascertained if there *are* any such nerves in the hide of a Doughface. More closely probably than that of any other bipedical animal, his cuticular membrane, in respect of imperviousness, resembles that of the rhinoceros.

Such are some of the anatomical idiosyncracies of the Doughface. What must be the physiological or functional peculiarities of an animal so organized, it is easy to predicate; since every animal is known to obey the laws of its physical organization. The Doughface, then, being organically, is therefore functionally, mean, mercenary, sycophantic, vacillating, treacherous, shameless, craven; and he is so, whatever may be the measure of his intellect, which, as I hinted, ranges, in different members of the race, from that of the monkey up to that of the man. Having only gristle to supply the place of a backbone, it is his nature to bend before every adverse breeze. With his enormous acquisitiveness, secretiveness and cautiousness; with his deficient firmness, self-esteem, and excessive limberness of the legs' central articulations, it is just as natural for him to

> "Crook the pregnant hinges of the knee,
> Where thrift may follow fawning,"

to offer himself in the political shambles; to quit a

sinking party for a rising one; to "hunt with the hound and run with the hare," as it is for the carrion crow to "prey on garbage." Why, he will run down an escaping slave, will "let slip the dogs of war" against such as would shelter the hunted bondsman; will betray his constituents; sell his country; rob his crippled grandmother of her crutch, to get an office, or, it may be, to put a dollar in his pocket. Yet, to give the poor devil his due, he is not a bad-natured fellow. He has no disinterested malevolence. Doubtless he would as soon do a good act as a bad one, if the former would pay as well. I said he is craven, cowardly. I will now add, that the nearest approach I ever knew one make to an exhibition of courage was on the occasion of his catching a chastisement from his better half, who, of course, either was *not* made of dough or had been fortunately baked to a healthy crustiness. I have read of another who, having been kicked down-stairs, was brave enough to say, "A man is not responsible for what takes place behind his back."

When that scornful Roanoke satirist placed his branding-iron on the base brows of this whole race of demagogues, he exclaimed, in slow, sharp, quaint intonations of voice so peculiarly his own, "It is not in our own strength that we of the South have always conquered you of the North. We have done it by using your own Doughfaces. Your Doughfaces! They are dirty dogs. They will eat dirty pudding."

And such are some of the physiological idiosyncracies of the Northern Doughface.

Optimism alleges a use for everything. It would

be interesting to hear an optimist define the use of a Doughface. Not that I deem it incredible that such a biped, amid the vast economies of the universe, may serve some purpose of utility. On the contrary, I have sometimes fancied I could designate his probable use. For it has occurred to me that the final cause of the Doughface may be to add a new argument to natural theology — to that branch of it especially which treats of the Divine Omnipotence. That argument, to state it within the narrowest compass, is this: "Since the Doughface, despite his abominable imitation of humanity, has yet the general exterior and shape of a man, his existence demonstrates the presence of an omnipotent force, because only such a force could so preserve the human form without the ordinary prerequisite of a soul." If the argument is sound, I would suggest — and I doubt not the heads of our theological seminaries will thank me for the suggestion — that a utilitarian purpose, one directly auxiliary to the great use which has been named, might be promoted by depositing specimens of the Doughface in the museums of those seminaries, and so bringing his characteristics within the immediate observation and study of all students in divinity.

So much for the Doughface. He is at once America's chief contribution to zoological science, and, as was intimated in the outset of this characterization of the species, the chief instrument, the tool employed by the slaveocracy now as heretofore, and especially now, in prosecuting its piratical schemes against the interests, the rights and the freedom of the people of the North.

CHAPTER VII.

MISCELLANEOUS NOTES FROM A COMMON PLACE BOOK.

SEPTEMBER 26, 1839.

I WAS in Boston attending an Anti-slavery meeting in Marlborough chapel, when John A. Collins put into my hands a letter from a vigilance committee in Richmond, Virginia, giving information of a couple of boys who were supposed to have been brought there by kidnappers from Lunenburg in this State. At C.'s request I entered into an investigation of the case. Taking a chaise, I proceeded directly to Lunenburg. Found a woman — Caza Hazard — in a meadow picking cranberries, and soon satisfied myself the boy was hers. Had William Little, of Shirley, Mass., immediately arrested as an accomplice in the crime, and taking him at once before Justice Brigham at Fitchburg, the further consideration of the case was postponed for a week or two. I found a Mr. Brown, who could identify the Hazard boy. Called on Gov. Everett, and requested that he would authorize an agent, under pay of the Commonwealth, to recover the boy.

The Governor thought he had no authority to do so. I referred to certain resolves of the last Legislature for authority. He ordered his secretary to hand him a copy of the acts of that body. "Yes, you are right," said he. "I will send any person you may think suitable." Mr. Brown, clothed with the State's authority, hastened to Richmond, and Mrs. Hazard, after a few days only, embraced her son again. I attended the trial of Little at Fitchburg at the time fixed, but the evidence against him not being conclusive, he was let off. The other boy also was recovered, and one or two of the kidnappers sent to our State prison. Though this was a somewhat troublesome service, yet its result was very satisfactory. It is not often one has an opportunity to give back to his mother her son that was lost. Those legislative resolves, too, under which, and by means of which, it was done, how delightful it was to think I had yielded no jot to the storm of opposition raised against them, when, single-handed, I urged their adoption by the Legislature ! It was then said by the opposition, that the resolves, if adopted, would do nobody any good. A few months later, and that poor mother and her son could tell those grave legislative lawyers a different story.

Brownson, whom I always love to read as I love to read almost no other American writer, be his opinions what they may, — and there is scarcely any opinion in the whole range of theology and metaphysics but he has advocated it at one time or another, — in his review for this month has a brief notice of Spooner's last work.

It goes pell-mell against all efforts for the removal of poverty. He maintains that poverty is a blessing.

He says, a greater than Spooner has said, "The poor ye have with you always."

I suspect it may yet be found by the reviewer that poverty of spirit and poverty of purse are two things.

Many good Catholics, I know, have sought poverty as a penance, as a means of reaching heaven, and they have given the testimony of their practice to the sincerity of their faith. I have a respect approaching veneration for such. But when shall we witness such a demonstration of honesty among our Protestant pastors of the blessings of poverty? If poverty *is* a blessing, it ought to be sought, and, most of all, by those who preach its blessedness. And if all efforts, such as Spooner's, to remove it, and to institute a more equal distribution of the means of subsistence, are of no avail, I should infer, either that there is no God, or that poverty *must* be a blessing. "As at present advised," *I* have no doubt it is an infernal evil, inferior only to sin itself, of which it is a most frequent occasion.

I have just as little doubt that every *true* man and woman will earnestly seek its removal.

Poor Haydon, the artist, has within the last few weeks committed suicide.

The papers have been much occupied with the case on this, as well as on his own side of the Atlantic. Only think of him, with his transcendent talents and genius, coming to such a conclusion from the force of sheer poverty, after a struggle of forty-two years! It is sickening. Is it not most remarkable, that of the several great men of wealth among his acquaintances, to whom, making known his circumstances, he applied for relief, Sir Robert Peel, though amid all the embarrassments consequent on the breaking up of his administration, should have been the only one to notice the application? That fifty pounds sent by Sir Robert (how gratefully it was noticed in poor Haydon's diary!) will do more to honor his name than all his public acts, beneficial as many of these, especially those of the last year of his government, are now so generally admitted to be. I have often wondered that he dared, single-handed and alone, to take up the cudgel against the Royal Academy. I suppose it was this that made him so poor, that finally killed him. There is a fine notice of him in yesterday's Boston "Daily Advertiser." I was not aware, until reading it, that he was so literary. Those notes, addressed separately to his wife, his daughter and his two sons, just before his departure, how affecting they are!

But was there not *something* wanting in his character that should have prevented such an exit?

July 8. — Called with friend Francis Jackson on Dr. and Mrs. Follen, at their home in Lexington. The Doctor was playing draughts with "Charley." They seemed very glad to see me, declaring they felt well acquainted with me from the interest with which they had observed my course in the Legislature. The Doctor spoke of "the time-serving clergy," adding, "The people would do better without than with them."

He referred to Martin Luther as a man of narrow mind and small intellect. He recalled some interesting incidents of his ministry in New York. Dr.

Dewey was once in the desk with him, when, for his allusion to slavery, a certain wealthy parishioner (of Dr. Dewey's) flung open his pew-door and left the church in a tempest of passion. After the sermon, Dr. Follen asked Dr. Dewey if he had said anything improper. "Nothing but *I* could have said," was Dr. Dewey's reply. "But he did not say he *would* have said it," added the Doctor. Afterwards, he said he thought his parishioner was as honest in rushing out of the church, as Dr. Follen was in uttering the sentiments he did.

He is a *man*, this Follen. I felt that this hour or two's conversation with him was worth living a twelvemonth for. What wonderful simplicity of manners! How apparently unconscious of his vast superiority!

Ralph Waldo Emerson. I heard his lecture on Genius. Horace Mann told me he deemed it the best he ever heard Emerson deliver; said it was a practical illustration of his subject. The calm, quiet beauty of his manner is remarkable. To hear him, is like walking in a garden of enchantment. If one does not always find philosophy in his speech, one is sure to find poetry.

I heard President Mahan of Oberlin to-night. He is *driving* preaching at a great rate. He spoke on the various grounds on which people hope to be saved. Thought he took for granted some things which it might have been well to prove. He imputed to Restorationists belief in salvation by purgatory. His manner is quite agreeable, but in energy very inferior to Finney's, as indeed is almost every other speaker's.

Heard Dr. Channing preach this morning. Text, "If any man be in Christ, he is a new creature." He denied that becoming a "new creature" implies the imparting of any new principle or faculty; spoke against the dogma of hereditary sin; alluded to the Anti-slavery movement as indicative of the growth and activity of Christianity. I was struck with the manner of his emphasis of the word *Anti-slavery*. There was in it a slight tone of defiance, as well as great earnestness.

July 1, 1839. — Friend Jackson drove me to-day to Quincy, to see John Quincy Adams, who gave us an hour of his rich conversation. He spoke of Shakspeare, phrenology, the marriage law, my course in the Legislature, &c. He thought we should sooner accomplish emancipation on his plan than on ours of immediatism. He said the law forbidding intermarriage of the races might as well not be. Still, women had better petition the Legislature for almost anything else than its repeal. Shakspeare's Othello was designed to show the strong natural repugnance to an amalgamation of whites and blacks; an opinion which he had stated to Fanny Kemble first in a conversation, and then in a letter to some friend. Miss Kemble was surprised he should have formed such an opinion of that play, and dissented from it altogether. *He* felt there could be no doubt of the repugnance itself. I asked if he had read Gall, Spurzheim or Combe on the subject of phrenology. He had not. "How could you write Dr. Sewall such a letter, then?" "Why, friend Sewall," said he laughingly, "sent me a copy of his book against

phrenology, and requested a letter from me on the
subject; and, wishing to oblige the Doctor, and
feeling in a mirthful mood, I sent him that letter."
The modern Brireus seemed in fine health and spirits.
I was much gratified with the visit.

1846. — J. G. WHITTIER.

On the 24th and 25th inst. I was at Amesbury,
going thither to deliver a lecture.   I have no recollection of satisfying myself less in any lecture than
in this, nor scarcely any of wishing to do better; for
Whittier himself was present, and I went thither by
his request, and it was my first lecture in Amesbury.
I spent the night at his home.   The family consists
of the poet, his mother and sister.   It was a treat to
me to pass a night with them.   John is one of the
greatest workers, politically even, in all our State.
I sometimes wonder how so fine a mind can stoop to
so much drudgery.   But Whittier has as much benevolence as he has ideality.   He knows the drudgery
must be done, and, since no one else does it, will do
it himself.   May Heaven bless him!   Heaven must
needs bless such a man.

It was in the vigor of early manhood that Salmon
P. Chase became the defender of freedom, and it was
in a city — Cincinnati, Ohio — where above all others
such a defence was most unpopular.   Suspicious
men condemned him then.   Selfish men charged him
with selfishness then.   But there he was, and there
he stood, a man in every sense of the word, defying

mobs and battling for freedom of speech and the press, deaf to personal appeals, heedless of personal popularity ; a friend of the outcast and downtrodden ; and party hate nor individual hate, nor any combination of both, nor all other hostile combinations, could hide his valor or taint his nobility of action.

The people of the State saw and acknowledged both ; and that portion of the people of the State who were determined to do what they could in behalf of freedom called upon him to lead them, and he did so. He became both their leader and teacher, and as such wrote out for them a platform and a creed which imbued the old parties with whatever positive element of freedom they possess.

Let none judge of either the courtesy or the ability. to appreciate worth of Massachusetts people in general, by the abuse of its Whig press towards Giddings, who visited the State for a purpose as pure and noble as ever hallowed prophet's mission. No ! there are multitudes of true men there worthy of the Pilgrims from whom they descended, who have done right worthy honor to the brave Ohioan. We know of one among them for whose nod of approbation, were we ambitious of applause, we would give more than for any number of plaudits however noisy, or any genuflections however profound, which it would be possible for the whole army of Hunkers to render, even if each possessed the lungs of Boreas and a facility of crooking "the pliant hinges of the knee " equalling that of a like number of Chinese mandarins.

We refer to James Russell Lowell, who has thus addressed the distinguished Ohioan :

" Giddings, far rougher names than thine have grown
    Smoother than honey on the lips of men ;
And thou shalt aye be honorably known
    As one who bravely used his tongue and pen,
As best befits a freeman — even for those
    To whom our Law's unblushing front denies
A right to plead against the life-long woes
    Which are the negro's glimpse of freedom's skies ;
Fear nothing and hope all things, as the right
    Alone may do securely ; every hour
The thrones of Ignorance and ancient Night
    Lose somewhat of their long-usurpéd power,
And freedom's lightest word can make them shiver,
With a base dread that clings to them forever."

Last evening I attended Professor Bush's reply to Emerson's lecture on Swedenborg. It was masterly, as it seemed to me, — triumphant. In regard to Emerson's objection to Swedenborg's doctrine that evils should be shunned as sins, and his assertion that it were better to shun them as evils, the professor made a witty as well as a philosophic remark. He said, in logic it was as if the mountain had brought forth a mouse ; but in mischief, as if the mouse had brought forth a mountain.

Dr. Hedge, in speaking of certain Abolitionists, at the Ritchie Hall meeting, said, "They are non-resistant Ishmaelites, who use the olive-branch for a war-club." I liked the expression. Was it not strong ?

Henry Clay. This distinguished Kentuckian draws near his end. We will speak no unkind word, therefore, of what he has failed to see, and seeing, failed to do. The morn of his manhood opened brightly in a noble endeavor to rid Kentucky of a giant wrong; and if its evening had been closed by a nobler struggle to perfect that endeavor, the sunset of his life would have been robed in glory. He has himself clouded that, and the name of Henry Clay, therefore, will never rank high in coming years among the benefactors of man.

Horace Mann's speech. This *is* refreshing. We had not fancied there was the material for such a speech in the brain of any American congressman. God be thanked for such a rebuke of our slowness to perceive! Our faith in congressional possibilities has been enlarged.

We were among those who regretted Mr. Mann's removal from the sphere in which he had so long labored as the Secretary of our Massachusetts Board of Education to a seat in the lower house of our National Legislature.

But this glorious speech of his, "on the right of Congress to legislate for the Territories of the United States, and its duty to exclude slavery therefrom," has wellnigh transformed all those regrets into sentiments of profound gratulation.

Indeed, if we may judge from this speech, he has changed not so much the nature as the theatre of his exertions. He is still laboring in the grand sphere of education, for which, perhaps, it were not extravagant to say, this single senatorial effort may do the work of a respectable university.

It must have stirred those stultified slaveholders in the House, and set some of them to thinking whether after all it is quite worth the while to fill up the present unpeopled regions of God's green earth with the victims of chattel slavery. We think it *must* have done this.

But if we mistake in so thinking, then it is certain that the resurrection trump would scarce startle the stupor of those tyrants. The speech abounds in felicitous and often startling illustrations for which the accomplished author is so remarkable. Was ever anything happier than his reference to those "lean kine" and "well-formed and fat-fleshed kine," those "seven thin ears blasted by the east wind," and the "seven ears of corn upon one stalk all rank and good," in contrasting the thrift of free labor with the unproductiveness of slave labor? But we almost regret this specification amid the many apt and striking contrasts and comparisons that throng the pages of this speech.

But we shall make such amends as we can for the indiscretion, by publishing as soon as possible the speech itself, which is hardly less distinguished by its skilful array of facts and its condensed expression of conclusive arguments, than by its beautiful imagery and its pat allusions. Inside or outside of the National House of Representatives it is the greatest speech we have yet seen on the subject, if not the greatest ever heard on any subject in either branch of the American Congress.

If the author would but rid himself of the trammels of those damnable "compromises of the Constitution" which even he admits to have forced the government of this great nation to be a colossal kidnapper, and take that instrument to demand no action inconsistent with the declared purposes of its glorious preamble, take it to be a charter of freedom, and no compact for the protection of unmitigated scoundrelism, — would Mr. Mann but do this, we should have one other speech from him which it would be worth one's while to travel half the circuit of the globe to hear, and that other speech would be "on the right" and the "duty" of the national government to *abolish* slavery throughout the land, and secure "to all the inhabitants thereof" the blessings of "a republican form of government."

December 11, 1851. — We notice some of our friends are anxious that Kossuth should express himself on the special question of freedom. Why should they be? Is not his life one eloquent defence of freedom? Is not his spirit full of the fire of liberty? Are not his teachings and all his speech and his very presence a sanctified and glorious embodiment of the doctrine of human brotherhood? For the United States, for the world, he stands far above the passions and petty schemes which cause the marshalling of parties and the planning of contests, and the contests themselves, as one of the world's *best* and purest master spirits, treading the path of a higher human freedom, and preparing the people everywhere to tread it with him. They who symbolize Shakspeare as the world-poet, ever place him in clearest sunshine and in the upper sky, above the region of the storm and tempest. He has within him the deepest springs of passion, feeling, imagination ; but he has, too, the power to control them, to be as still amid the stormiest outbreak as if he heard it not. And the world-master, like the world-poet, must stand above the jar and din of the strifes of the day, either to understand them, or to guide and control. And this is Kossuth's position.   From him, therefore, we would ask no word for any party, whether that party be for or against freedom.   From him we would seek no expression, if we could surely get it, which would cause him to favor this or that political division in our country.   Let him plead for Hungary and her freedom with his whole soul, as no other living man can, and he will do more for liberty, the world over, than he would by any other course.   Let him do that untrammelled, and with every free sympathy centring round and in him, and he will do more for freedom in our land than any American could accomplish.

Said Edmund Burke, after he had had some experience of both the cost and the worth of fame, "I greatly deceive myself if I would give a peck of refuse wheat for all that is called fame and honor in the world." What the master statesman had learned by so painful a tuition, every poet, we take it, must needs know by intuition. He who lives *only* for fame, labors, be it never so unconsciously, but to deserve infamy, and will get it one day if progress is a law of humanity.

Whittier's Poems. A splendid edition of these
has lately been published by Mussey, and a notice
of it, and of its glorious author, by James Russell
Lowell. If it takes a poet to appreciate a poet,
Lowell has certainly one of the conditions precedent
to an appreciation of Whittier; else almost everybody fibs about the former. We know nothing of
poetry as an art, and would as soon think of taking
the psychological dimensions of Emanuel Swedenborg, whom Ralph Waldo Emerson said it would
take a population of philosophers to comprehend,
as of criticising the poetic productions of John
Greenleaf Whittier. We can judge of them only
as the good woman judged of the Bible. She knew
it to be a good book, because she felt it to be so.
We feel Whittier's verse to be good; and if, as we
have heard some affirm, it is not always conformable
to the canons of criticism, we would, we had almost
said, have those canons conformed to it; just as
that good woman declared that facts contradictory
of the scriptures should be made to conform to them.
We know not, and care not, whether Whittier uses
the file and the burnisher so assiduously as they are
employed by a Bryant or a Longfellow. But we do
know that his verse stirs our blood as it was never
stirred by any other American poet. We have committed to memory more of his poetry than of any
other living author's.

And if we ever find our zeal in the cause of reform
flagging, we have but to recall some of those live
lines of his, and straightway it is all on fire again.
How a man can read Whittier at all, and not bestir

himself in behalf of humanity, is one of the things past our finding out.

In truth, no *man* can do so, though bipeds in the form of men may, and sometimes do. Lowell says Whittier's poetry "gains by reciting." So does his own. And does not Shakspeare's also?

There is one thing about *Horace Greeley* we like. He is an American. Not in name, not by birth, but *in heart;* and whether in Naples or Rome, London or Paris, he is thoroughly true, unaffectedly but boldly open in defence of every just principle peculiar to our Republic. He makes no terms with titles, and is not caught, as so many weak Americans are, by the glare of their tinsel. And we will answer for it, it was not my Lord Doolittle or my Lady Dash whom Horace Greeley sought, but *Mazzini* and those Doers for Humanity, in Europe, whether titled or untitled, who are scoffed by the proud as "adventurers," and denounced by the "great" as "demagogues."

A friend of ours, not a political ally of Mr. Greeley, yet fully able to appreciate him, wrote to us some months ago that "no American had produced a happier effect in Europe, among the many able and distinguished men who had met him, by his simplicity, intelligence and manliness, and especially by the modesty, yet sagacious firmness, with which, when it was proper to do so, he defended whatever was right and really great in the American character and republic."

We rejoice when such citizens visit Europe, and

we regard it as a most fortunate circumstance for both sides of the water when they give their impressions of what they saw and felt when abroad.

Miss Elizabeth Blackwell, M.D. We learn from a brief yet highly complimentary notice of this lady in the "New York Tribune" that she has lately returned to that city and commenced the practice of her profession "at No. 44 University Place," after an absence of two years in Europe, "one of which was spent as an *interne* or house physician at the Maternity Lying-in Hospital," and the other "in the same capacity in the St. Bartholomew's Hospital in London." Miss Blackwell has also spent some time with Preisnitz at Graefenburg, studying the water-cure.

From what we chance to know of "Dr. Blackwell," we do not hesitate to predict that, despite of her sex, she will take a high rank in the profession for which she has qualified herself by so many years of hard study, and against obstacles which would have appalled a woman of ordinary courage and self-reliance. Apart from the excellence of her scientific attainments, she is a woman of intellect, of taste, of liberal culture, and of rare amiableness, itself a noble quality in a physician. She is also a good writer in both prose and verse. The appearance of such a woman among the doctors should be welcomed as a blessing by both sexes, and especially by her own. We hope the day is not very far distant in which the honors, the services and the emoluments of the medical profession will be largely shared by "the better half" of creation. We hail with pleasure the efforts we have observed in various directions to hasten the advent of that day.

Massachusetts has her full proportion of strong men, but it has not a stronger one than Judge Charles Allen, nor one more beloved by those who know him. He is a rare exception to the old proverb that "a prophet is not without honor save in his own country ;" for the judge is decidedly — and to the praise of that city be it remarked — the most popular man in Worcester, the renowned "heart" of his native Commonwealth. We have had the honor of knowing Judge Allen for many years, and always have we delighted to contemplate him as one of the few men of big brains with hearts to match them. He belongs to the small category of great men. It is not, therefore, a thing at all remarkable that we never knew him attacked with either virulence or ability sufficient to provoke a defence of himself, but great good was the result. For some years past, beginning with the surrender of Whiggism to General Taylor, we have not failed to observe others' rascalities have been his grandest occasions of usefulness. And the end of these, we will venture to predict, is not yet, if there shall be found grit enough in the coming Congress to give him that long-desiderated committee of investigation.

Spooner's "Unconstitutionality of Slavery" is so great a work that we have never dared attempt a review of it — and we intend no such attempt. We have felt, and feel, that neither our brain nor our paper is big enough to justify such an attempt.

It is a work, as N. P. Rogers said, to make one's "head ache" in the reading, if one will so read it as to understand its meaning, which, so far as we know, almost no one has yet done.

It is a work, too, as that same clear-headed and great-hearted lawyer declared, containing so much of legal erudition and labor as, if expended in efforts to bolster up popular rascality, or to defend doubtful cases of rich clients, would have made the author's fortune and won for him a wide present fame.

It is a work which *we* do not believe any man can read and appreciate, and ever after be found driving his pen or wagging his tongue in defence of what are so mischievously called the pro-slavery compromises of the Constitution, unless such a man's rottenness of heart shall quite equal the magnitude of his brain.

Professor Mitchell. This distinguished astronomer has his hands full. He is, we hear, to be professor at Albany — to have an eye on the observatory building there, and over the one built in Cincinnati. In addition he is to give a portion of his time to the St. Louis and Cincinnati Railway. Did you ever see the professor? He is very small in stature; but he is all energy, and there is no such thing as "tire" in him. He can sleep anywhere, eat anything, work night and day, write, lecture, and be always as fresh as any mortal we may meet. Take him off a heavy day's survey, and he will discourse at night on astronomy with a stirring eloquence.

Such is the professor; and if any man can, he will get through unquestionably with whatever engagements he may make, be they ever so numerous.

Carlyle " complains in the bitterness of his heart that the true kings and governors of mankind have retired in disgust from the task of governing the world, and betaken themselves to the altogether private business of governing themselves. Whenever the world at large shall become as wise as they, when all men shall be content to govern themselves merely, then, and not till then, will ' the true constitution of government' begin to be installed." Alas! then, for " the good time coming," it will not suffice to " wait a little longer." We wish he had told us by what means " the world at large " may be made " as wise " as those " true kings and governors of mankind," who have retired in " such disgust from the task of governing the world, and betaken themselves to the " so much worthier " business of governing themselves." And this is what he promises to do in what is yet to come from his pen.

Politics are inseparable from what of morality, of religion, of humanity, there is in us, and always should make those the instrument or the servant of these.

In a community its politics are an outbirth, a correspondence, an expression or a manifestation of either its morals, its faith, its enlightenment or its vices, its unbelief, its selfishness and its ignorance.

The actual work of a community, as such, the doings, that is to say, of the government of a community, together with the science of that work of those doings, constitute its politics; though it is, with reference to deeds, exclusive of all science or theory, that we for the most part employ the word politics. In themselves, therefore, politics are neither a good nor an evil; but they are either, or both, just according to the nature of the principles and the character of the deeds composing them. It is folly, therefore, to prate, as many do, against politics and politicians, as if these were, in themselves, infernal. It is of a piece with the fanaticism that would rail against art and artists, or against religion and religionists. For myself, I never wish to live in the same house with even a woman taking no interest in politics — and for the same reason that I would not live with one devoid of a heart or a brain.

While we would strenuously insist that the mother's influence should be for good upon her family, we shall as positively insist that man shall allow woman to place herself in a situation, if she insists, to use and to hold a good influence. She must not be ever, as she is now, by law, custom and public opinion, held as an inferior and subservient. Now let her teaching be ever so true and holy, the father may, if he pleases, counteract all those teachings by both precept and example, or he may remove the child from her influence.

We know some "respectable" people, who, while they would shrink with virtuous abhorrence from the thought of picking a man's pocket, will not hesitate to lie to you.

One will promise to dine with you at one o'clock,

and leave you and your household to "wait for him" until one and a half of the clock. A bootmaker tells you your boots shall be sent to you on Saturday evening, but you see nothing of them till the night of the following Monday.

By your landlady's "regulations," the hour of breakfast is six and a half o'clock; but she keeps you waiting until near seven, which, unless to escape lying yourself, you resolve to go, as in such a case you should go, breakfastless, makes you disappoint a dozen persons whom you had promised to see at seven, and these in their turn a hundred others.

The house-painter promises to grain for you in the morning a room which you constantly occupy. You turn its furniture topsy-turvey, and thus make ready for his hour's work. You stand waiting to receive him twice that length of time, and wait in vain. At night you send to inquire the reason of his non-appearance, and are told he "will surely come in the morning."

The parson, from "the sacred pulpit," announces that his lecture on the important subject of the office and character of Melchisedek, "will commence at half-past seven precisely." You repair to the church, but find "the service" commences not until some ten long minutes after the time appointed.

The catalogue might, for aught we know, be swelled to the magnitude of the Bodleian library. All these "respectable" people are liars, and as such would be shunned by decent Turks the world over; for the Turks, we believe, are a truth-telling people. And these "respectable" people are pickpockets as well as liars. Their lying involves stealing, for it robs you of your time, and "time is money." And worse are they than ordinary pickpockets, for to the theft they perpetrate they add the sin of violating your confidence, which the common thief never betrays.

CHAPTER VIII.

LETTERS.

MR. BRADBURN'S correspondence was large, embracing men and women eminent in reforms, politics, theology and literature.

No letters of those now living — save one of condolence — will be published in this memorial, and a few only of those who preceded or have since followed him into the next life. He kept no copies of his own letters, and I have requested none of friends or others. Those of his given in this chapter were copied by myself.

I have added the one of Mr. Garrison's and the Dorchester petitioners — which properly belong in another chapter — to this collection, for convenience.

[To Nathaniel P. Rogers, Esq.]

BOSTON, October 8, 1846.

DEAR ROGERS, — I am in the midst of packing for a visit to Cleveland, Ohio, intending to leave here tomorrow morning, to be absent I know not how long, but doubtless through the coming winter. But I cannot leave without a word to you. And yet I fear you will not be able to read it, perhaps not to hear it read. For last Saturday, Dr. Kittredge, who had just returned from your place, told me you were not essentially better. I would have arranged to visit you if I had not feared my deafness would probably occasion you injury. Yet there is nothing I could *say* that would be likely to alleviate the evils of your illness or help you to bear them. But it would do *me* good to talk with you, were it possible, especially at this time. You are very often in my thoughts; and thoughts of you always give me pleasure. It pleases me to think of your noble, self-sacrificing efforts in behalf of humanity; of how these many long years you have so constantly gone for "humanity first." But you were the last man I should think of telling such efforts can never be lost, that never was a right thing done nor a true word uttered, but "humanity" was blessed by it. I rejoice, and I think you may rejoice, that you were able to make the sacrifices requisite to the saying of so much truth, and the doing of so much good, as you have said and done.

I hear many inquiries made for your health, and many expressions of honest regret that you should be housed up, even for a season, from persons capable of admiring genius and reverencing the spirit of self-sacrifice and devotion to truth. John G. Whittier often speaks of you in words of truest sympathy and tender affection. I was at his house a week since. Lysander Spooner said to me the other day, "I wish Rogers might know the exalted respect I have for him." It delights me to hear different persons, as well those who reject as those who accept your cherished peculiarities of opinion, thus uniting to speak kindly and admiringly of you; and I cannot help telling you of it. But it is on their account, rather than on yours, that I am so delighted; for the thing speaks well of themselves, since next to being and doing, I rank the capacity of appreciating those who are and do.

When friends tell me they fear your work is about done, I tell them, no! such a man's work will never be done; for "humanity" will always be, and N. P. Rogers will be always working for it. If he "passes on," departs from our presence here, he will find larger means of doing his favorite work. Such, at least, is my hope. I have no idea of limiting a man by the accidents of time and space. It is a common notion that a man's work will endure forever; but I believe he may work forever.

Dear Rogers, I don't know that we shall ever see each other more in the flesh. For you are very ill, I am going to Ohio, and what is called life is ever so uncertain. But so far forth as we love the good and the true, we shall be near to each other in the highest and best sense of that expression. But while we are on the earth, I desire to hear from you occasionally. And until you become able — if you ever are again — to hold a pen, may I not hope that your dearer self, or one of your dear children, will once in a while drop me a line.

I am, as I have ever been since "we were first acquaint,"

Affectionately yours,

GEORGE BRADBURN.

To N. P. ROGERS, Esq., Plymouth, New Hampshire.

[To Hon. Charles Sumner.]

CLEVELAND, May 25, 1856.

DEAR SIR, — The blood boiled in my veins as I read at the breakfast-table on the 23d inst. the telegraphic account of the assault made on your person, in the afternoon preceding, by the ruffianly Brooks. And, for the moment at least, I was quite divested of any non-resistant feelings I may have had, and almost of those specific inclinations which some of your own writings are so well calculated to inspire; and wished that the friends of freedom in our great National Bear Garden might be always prepared to meet the myrmidons of despotism in the latter's own way and with their own weapons. I wish, however, that you may have been enabled to "possess your soul" in as much patience as would befit a true man under the infliction of so atrocious an outrage. Nay, I believe that you have been so enabled; and therefore I must needs congratulate you on having finally suffered, and so suffered, for the cause which your eloquence had done so much to prosper. In other times, — I had fancied *such* times were past, — it was my privilege (for privilege I have ever esteemed it) to encounter on many occasions assassins armed with bowie-knives, revolvers and cowhides; and although on those occasions I was in momentary expectation of "sudden death," from which all good churchmen so earnestly pray to be delivered, yet I assure you that by "the grace of God," by my faith in the righteousness of our cause and in the efficiency of the blood of martyrs, they were among the happiest occasions of my life.

The heaviest blows which have yet been struck for humanity were just those which have been inflicted upon your head, though the cowardly Carolinian meant them for only "his native State." Your speech, which was the occasion, though by no means the cause, of those blows, is a grand thing. Senator Crittenden — so Giddings, who called on me the other day on his way home, told me — pronounced it the ablest effort he ever listened to in either house of Congress. That speech has quickened the pulse of every lover of freedom throughout the land ; but the blows of that South Carolina "Thug" have awakened in the masses an intensity of indignation against the slaveocracy which a thousand speeches, each as stirring as that, would have been powerless to produce. My dear sir, let *that* be your consolation, whatever else may come of those blows.

A large meeting was held last evening in this city to express the feelings of our citizens in regard to this outrage. It was called at the suggestion of Judge Rufus P. Spaulding, than whom anti-Nebraskaism has not an abler advocate in Ohio. I was glad to say a few words in that meeting, and never before felt so deeply the need of such a tongue as yours.

I am most truly yours,
GEORGE BRADBURN.

To the Hon. CHARLES SUMNER.

[To Mrs. Gerrit Smith.]

MELROSE, May 5, 1875.

MY DEAR MRS. SMITH, — Ever since the words "Gerrit Smith is dead" flashed to the country, invoking such universal sympathy for the great bereavement which has come so suddenly to yourself and yours, I have wanted to write you. But hitherto I have not been *able* to do so. Nor is it now, or ever will be, in my power to write such a letter as I would like to send you.

I have at least one satisfaction : I am sure you will have needed no assurances from either Frances or me of our thorough sympathy with you, and with all belonging to you, in this affliction ; for you know us both too well not to have felt that you had it.

An old English divine says, in substance, that he who sympathizes with the sorrowing helps bear their burden, taking part of it upon himself. I believe it. So how should I not have "taken some comfort" in thinking of an almost unwonted alleviation which must have attended your sorrow. For when were more or tenderer expressions of sympathy ever called forth by a like event than were elicited by the departure of your other self from this world of shadows to the *real* world? And I further believe — as probably that good English parson did not — that sympathy helps its objects even when not expressed. So, too, and in virtue of the same spiritual law, I believe our friends who have entered the causal world may serve us there effectually, very likely more so than they could have done by remaining longer in this world of effects, and none the less certainly because we may be unconscious of their aid. And I do wish, my dear friend, that these "articles of faith" may be yours too, and afford you as much comfort in this

hour of your greatest need as they have frequently
given me.

Some eminent men have won my admiration, some
my affection, some my veneration.   But Gerrit
Smith was among the "precious few" whom I have
alike admired, loved and revered.   I met him first
in 1837, at an anti-slavery convention in New York
city.   I was struck at sight with his fine person, the
finest I thought I had ever seen, excepting perhaps
that of Daniel Webster.   And having heard him often,
and become intimately acquainted with him, I concluded Swedenborg need not have wished a better
illustration of his favorite science of correspondences.

In the course of an acquaintance of more than
thirty-five years with your husband, I do think, and
will say it at the risk of seeming egotistical, that I
learned to appreciate him.   I saw him under various
circumstances, — in your own beautiful home many
times, — corresponded with him, and more freely than
with any other person of eminence, not excepting
Salmon P. Chase; travelled with him, discussed
with him questions in the press, in conventions and
other public assemblies wherein exciting questions
were wont to be earnestly, some would say furiously,
debated.   And though we sometimes differed, we
never quarrelled.   Neither did either ever utter one
word or entertain a thought in derogation of the
other's honesty or honor.   Considering his social position, his political theories and personal practice,
considering also the meaning of democracy — a term
worse prostituted among us than any other in our
vocabulary — I think he was the best democrat I ever

knew. I think, too, that no man on this continent ever did more for human rights. He had a grand abhorrence of oppression — loving liberty because he loved man. His "indignation and wrath" against unrighteousness was truly Paul-ine; yet his compassion for "every soul of man that doeth evil" was extra-Paul-ine — and so he went bail for "Jeff" Davis.

I can never be too grateful for the gift of his friendship. The life of such a man makes me think better of "this present evil world;" and, now that he has gone hence, will add a new attraction to "the world to come." But I had hoped to see him again here. And, during the year which has just closed, I often said to F., "I *must* make Gerrit Smith another visit," and have one more comparison of notes with him while there is yet time. But, alas for myself! that was not to be.

I pray you to remember us affectionately as well as sympathizingly to your sole son, your only daughter, her husband and their children; and believe that we are Truly yours and theirs,

GEORGE BRADBURN.

To Mrs. GERRIT SMITH, Peterboro', New York.

DORCHESTER, April 3, 1839.

Mr. GEORGE BRADBURN.

Honored and Respected Sir, — In view of the essential service you have rendered the cause of virtue and humanity by your course in the Legislature, we tender to you our sincere thanks and heartfelt gratitude; but realize at the same time our total inability to make an adequate return for your able defence of our characters and the advocacy of the object of our petition.

We are sorry that any among us should be so alarmed by pro-slavery influence as to withdraw their names from the petition in the hour of trial, and thus leave you and the cause of impartial liberty to the mercy of base assailants. But, dear sir, you are not and will not be forsaken by the true friends of humanity. No, never, never will you be forgotten by us while memory holds her empire, and while we have hearts to feel for the woes of millions of our brothers and sisters suffering under the rod of oppression. That God may reward you a hundred-fold in this life, and in the world to come with life everlasting, will be our humble prayer.

Please accept the enclosed certificate as a lasting memorial of our gratitude for what you have done to aid and sustain us in our hallowed enterprise.

Signed in behalf of the Dorchester Female Antislavery Society.

SARAH BAKER,
Corresponding Secretary.

[From William Lloyd Garrison.]

BOSTON, April, 1840.

MY DEAR BRADBURN, — Your note of yesterday, requesting letters of introduction to anti-slavery friends in England, has just come. As you intimate that you may leave to-morrow, and Francis Jackson informs me that he has a bundle for you, you see I have scarcely a moment to comply with your request. But George Thompson will be sufficient to obtain for you an introduction to a host of noble men and women across the Atlantic. How glad, how *very* glad, I am that Lucretia Mott and her husband are going to the convention! And how sorry, how *very* sorry, I am that I cannot go with them and you! My dear Bradburn, it is not probable that I shall arrive in season to be at the opening of the convention; but, I beseech you, *fail not to have women recognized as equal beings in it.* Interchange thoughts with dear Thompson about it. I know he will go for humanity, irrespective of sex. God speed you!

Your friend,   WM. LLOYD GARRISON.

[From Edmund Quincy, Esq.]

DEDHAM, March 4, 1842.

DEAR FRIEND, — I have just received your letter, and hasten to reply that we shall be most happy to have you here on the evenings you name. You will, of course, come to my house on your arrival. You must have spoken to some purpose at Salem to have produced such flattering results. It seems the age of brickbats and rotten eggs is not yet passed. It is, indeed, one and the same thing with the age of American chivalry. I cannot promise you so warm a reception here. I think *even you* would find it hard to move the stones in Dedham's streets to testify against you. I cannot flatter you that your advent will cause any advance in the egg-market. Whatever your future may have in this particular, the Abolitionists here will be right glad to see you and to hear you; and foremost among them will be

Your friend,   EDMUND QUINCY.

[From Hon. Salmon P. Chase.]

CINCINNATI, July 4, 1849.

My DEAR BRADBURN, — I thank you for your kind
letter. I am right glad that my election gratified
you. As to the bargain, the substance of it was that
the Democratic and Independent Freesoilers preferred to help the Democrats rather than the Whigs.
They formed an alliance, therefore, to this extent,
neither requiring the other to abandon any principle.
In fact, as to matters of principle, all that was necessary was for the Democrats to prove themselves
progressive, and advance in the line of their own
fundamental ideas, and they could not be long in
arriving at the position occupied by the Freesoilers.
There is need enough for both to advance from the
highest position either has reached. But then you
must not find fault if we seem to advance slowly.
Remember that while you and others, unencumbered
by organizations, ascend easily into the sphere of a
perfect polity, we poor practical fellows are dragging
along this huge world wain to which we are hitched
by party traces and can ascend not so easily! Make
allowance for the fiction, I beseech you, dear friend.
I think I have some such ideas as your own — at
least in some respects — as to what is desirable, what
ought to be striven for, what may be, perhaps, some
day attained. But let us hasten slowly, never forgetting, however, to hasten. Think what it cost to
make a Phidian Jove even out of Parian marble!
What measurings, and cuttings, and blockings, and
clippings, and chisellings, and polishings! At last,

behold the God! And even before the block was
cut out of the quarry, what long ages to make the
marble by the sure processes which the wisdom of the
Infinite has established as the laws of nature! Let
us believe the truth, and proclaim it, the highest truth
we can reach; but let us not be discouraged or complain if we find ourselves unable, after all, to do more
than bring the masses along with us at a very moderate pace.

Don't you remember that I once told you I was a
Liberty man because I was a Democrat? Well, this
little sentence explains my whole action since. I
have ever been anxious to prevent the Liberty party
from receiving too large an infusion of conservatism
— anxious to have it cherish Democratic sympathies
and principles. I was glad, therefore, when the
opportunity of uniting with it a large portion of the
radical Democracy of the country, and also a large
portion of the most liberal and progressive Whigs,
presented itself. Hence my labors to perfect this
union at Buffalo. It was because I thought I saw
the signs of this coming opportunity that I was unwilling to have any nomination made by the Liberty
party in 1847. I hope for the best results from the
organization of the fused elements of Libertyism and
radical Democracy, and progressive Whiggism in the
free Democracy. What results will actually arise, —
whether my hope will be fulfilled or disappointed, —
the future will reveal. Of one thing only I can assure
you. I am *still* a Liberty man, because I am a Democrat. I am still resolute in the determination not to
rest satisfied until every legitimate and constitutional

power of the government shall be put in action against slavery, because slavery is inconsistent with the great democratic idea of equal rights among men.

I have a sort of presentiment that I shall meet you at Cleveland; if so, this letter will hardly reach Boston before your departure. I anticipate a great gathering on the 13th.

The cholera is absolutely fearful in its ravages here. Near nine hundred died last week, and the number of deaths this week will probably exceed a thousand. Its ravages are greatest among the poor emigrants, who are crowded together in miserable quarters, and who cannot be persuaded, I am told, to observe the least caution. Oh, how loudly does this visitation call on us to make better provision for labor! When there is enough and to spare for all God's creatures, how sad that the millions perish for lack of such knowledge, and lack of the ordinary comforts of life, while the few are surrounded with all the appliances of luxury! I am thankful that my own condition is one of ease and comfort; and yet I feel as if it were almost criminal to enjoy it while so many suffer such sad extremes of wretchedness and destitution. When shall we have a just organization of society and labor? Never, I fear, till *Christian principle* is far more generally diffused among all classes.

I hope I have not wearied you. Write me as often as you can, as often as the spirit moves you, assured that your letters will always be welcome to

Your friend,
S. P. CHASE.

[From Hon. Gerrit Smith.]

PETERBORO', January 18, 1850.

DEAR BRADBURN, — I thank you for your *visit* to me. You remember my telling you that none of my correspondents succeeded to anything like the extent you do in putting *themselves* into their letters. A letter from Bradburn is a *visit* from Bradburn.

Well, — to the convention. C. C. Burleigh, Foster, Pillsbury, Remond, Douglass, &c., were there. One whole day was set apart for Burleigh and me to discuss the constitutional question. I felt bound to discuss it as a purely legal question. Burleigh, on the other hand, discussed it mainly as a historical question. Of course I availed myself largely of Lysander Spooner's argument; and when, after having characterized that manly and invincible argument as it deserved to be characterized, I added that were I studious of fame or usefulness I had rather be the author of that argument than of any other law argument ever written, either on this side or the other of the Atlantic, there was surprise in the large audience. Lawyers, clergymen, merchants and politicians were present. I wish you had been there. The vote stood 5 to 1 in favor of my interpretation of the law.

I have frequently written out a speech before delivering it, more frequently when a young man than of late years. But I have a miserable *verbal* memory. It would take me a week to commit a speech to memory; and even then I should not get it half right. My friends think I speak better when I speak altogether without preparation. I do not agree with them, however.

Yes! I *have* noticed in the papers my slow and lazy utterance, compared with that of most public speakers. We all laughed at your making my short sentences models for a man in the last stage of the asthma.

In reply to your request, I have to say that I have never kept an account of my donations. I never would consent to keep it. I came very easily by my large possessions. Not to part with them as easily would be both disgraceful and wicked. Should I spend half a day in taxing my recollections and adding up my *principal* gifts in money in aid of the cause of freedom, I should, probably, be quite wide of the mark. I suppose they would exceed a hundred thousand dollars. My gifts to help persons get homes, — in *money*, perhaps, not more than half so great. My gifts to other objects amounting to less than a hundred thousand dollars. From first to last I have, also, given away some two hundred thousand acres of land. But while a little of this land was good and valuable, most of it was inferior and low-priced. I am called a very benevolent man. But my benevolence seldom rises to self-sacrifice.

When, my dear friend, are you coming to visit us again, bringing your good wife with you? There is room in our home and in our hearts for you. My wife sends love to yours, and to yourself.

Truly yours,

GERRIT SMITH.

[From Hon. Joshua R. Giddings.]

WASHINGTON CITY, May 19, 1856.

DEAR BRADBURN, — Thanks for your letter. The circumstances attending my speech have developed some new views; and as you are interested to know all about it, I will tell you how it occurred. My feelings were aroused on looking into the questions involved. I found that our committee on ways and means, with Campbell at its head, had been defeated. The corruption involved in the bill before me was great, as you will see by my speech. I had fairly got under way when Campbell interrupted me. I could have answered him any question, but he insisted on explaining when I knew no explanation could be made. Yet I was constrained to be civil. I therefore was compelled to *suppress* the emotions of my soul. This threw upon the brain such a pressure, as to deprive me of consciousness. I fell, and when I revived I found myself under way out of that hall, borne by the arms of kindness and friendship. Now, sir, I give you notice that I do not expect you to say, that I fainted under an effort to be *civil* to a doughface. If you attack me on that point, I won't promise any forbearance whatever. But the transaction has demonstrated most effectually the mode by which a doughface may attack a lover of liberty.

Another point in philosophy has thus been developed in direct contradiction to our old notions. In past times it has been regarded as dangerous to speak. Now, the danger is shown to consist in *silence*. It was right for you to express your views in regard to

President ———. What is duty for me is not duty
for you. I am here before the country in an official
and representative capacity. The position I hold
should be used to promote the objects and interests
of those who conferred it.

I think we shall elect our candidate, whoever he
may be, if he takes position on our platform. But I
think the friends of Fremont have grossly neglected
the bringing out of his views on the right and duty
of Congress to exclude slavery from our territories.
Without a full committal on that point he will be
defeated.

But now for the work before us. We have much
to do this year, for the work of regenerating the nation must go on until we are redeemed from oppression.

In my opinion, your excellence as an editor consists
not in your severity nor in your mildness. Your
force and power consist in the peculiar type of your
own mind. Neither Wade, nor Chase, nor I, nor any
human being, can change or make it better. If I
were to advise you in anything, it would be to give
scope to your own thoughts, express your own views,
utter your own sentiments, let them flow just as
they gush from the heart. Away with dictation! I
would not trust any mortal man to give utterance to
my thoughts; and I know if I were to utter yours,
or attempt it, I should mar their beauty. No, my
dear friend, while I am always happy to listen to
friends and to have advice and suggestions from them,
I have found from long experience that God has
given me judgment and conscience and feeling to

guide me, and I never surrender that judgment without incurring self-condemnation afterwards. That principle applies to all men ; and if you go into the paper, act yourself fully and untrammelled.

Remember me to Mrs. Bradburn. Mrs. G. and Maria send love. Your friend,

J. R. GIDDINGS.

[From Rev. John Pierpont.]

WASHINGTON CITY, December 22, 1864.

DEAR FRIEND,—I have not answered your last kind letter before, for two reasons ; first, impaired health ; and, secondly, I had not found time to finish Renan's book, "The Life of Jesus." The book appears to me to be rather a strange medley of learning, scepticism and orthodoxy. He is well acquainted with all sorts of out-of-the-way books, especially the rabbinical. He cuts up the evangelists, hip and thigh, making no bones of making legends out of what others have regarded veritable history, and yet talks without the least wryness of a "resurrected *God*." Yet I have found it an interesting book, and to me instructive. I think he would have made a better book had he not ignored or slightly esteemed the *miraculous facts of spiritualism* that in this country, and in Europe too, are continually taking place before our eyes. We certainly *do* see diseases healed by the laying on of hands, — chronic organic diseases, — as remarkable as any related in the New Testament. I don't know whether or not you believe this, but *I do know it* to the same extent that I know *any* historical fact of which I become an eye-witness. How do these

cures differ from those of the New Testament?
Shall we shut our eyes to these facts and think we
thereby annihilate them? "I tell you, nay." It is
not so easy a thing to annihilate *a fact*. To be sure,
a cure is not always effected. But the fact that a
man does *not* cure in one case does not *touch the
fact* that he did cure in another. The disciples of
Jesus didn't always succeed. In one case of their
failure, they wanted to know *why*. The Teacher told
them, first, from their want of faith, and secondly,
their want of knowledge. They didn't *know* that
"this kind goeth not out but by prayer and fasting."

I am not troubled about the *miracles* of the New
Testament. It is the *definition* of the miracle that I
boggle at. Our Orthodox friends begin with defini-
tions which suit their purpose, and defining a miracle
thus, — "a violation or suspension of a law of nature,"
—then say, "None but God can counteract or suspend
the laws of nature, which are his own laws; Jesus
Christ, you admit, did work *miracles:* therefore
Jesus Christ *is* God." To this, I reply, "if God
means to have us observe his laws and keep them,
depend upon it, he will not set us the example of
violating them himself." His laws are like himself,
"the same yesterday, to-day and forever." Define
a miracle as etymology defines it, — "something
rather wonderful," — and the difficulty all vanishes;
not necessarily "a manifestation of divine power,"
but *the manifestation of a power not hitherto recognized by those to whom the act in question is a
wonder.*

Then, again, Renan need not have spoken so glibly

of a "resurrected God" if he had not ignored the
great doctrine of Spiritualism, that every one has his
resurrection soon after the spirit leaves the body, in
the act that we call death.

St. Paul very distinctly tells us that "there is a
natural body, and there is a spiritual body." It was
the *spiritual* body of Jesus that rose, and they who
saw him rise were endowed, for the time, with the
power of *spirit vision;* a power that has been recognized under certain conditions, physical or mental,
the world over, all history through. In our own
day there are hundreds who at times possess that
power. I know some who have the power of seeing
the spirit body, others recognize its presence without seeing it. My own great-grandfather, my father,
my mother, my son, my daughter-in-law, have been
heard, seen, and so described to me that there could
be no mistake by as many different "seers," who
could have known nothing of the animal body which
the spiritual body left behind it.

Thus, my friend, my faith has increased in the
marvellous, or, if you please, in the miraculous facts
of sacred history, as the sphere of my knowledge of
anthropology has extended.

Pray excuse me from discussing any other subject
till another opportunity.

Love to your better half.

Very truly yours,

JOHN PIERPONT.

[From Mrs. Lucretia S. Mott.]

PHILADELPHIA, 4 mo., 12, 1841.

MY DEAR GEORGE BRADBURN, — I have often been
surprised that so many months have passed without
either my better James or myself filling a sheet for
thy perusal. Thine was truly acceptable, — compliments and all.

All thou says of that delightful Irish band in Dublin we most heartily respond to. If thou could see
how enthusiastic we are when speaking of them, and
what long letters have passed between us, thou would
think our love for them almost equal to thine. Indeed, towards England and Scotland too there is a
drawing cord of love which makes us wish to forget
that narrow pass of their character, and remember
only the noble highway which we were privileged to
travel. There are some lovely spirits in that fatherland, and I shall ever rejoice that we have been there
and that we found such ready access to their generous hearts. I wish thou wast here to participate in
the joy when a parcel is received from over the water. Indeed, I have often wished thou could find
profitable exercise of thy talents in this goodly city
of ours. Massachusetts Legislature needs thee too,
and perhaps, at no distant day, Washington will be
honored, or to speak more as becometh "one of us,"
favored with and benefited by thy presence.

We were obliged for the paper containing an account of thy visit to Father Matthew. It interested
us much. Have we a greater miracle on record than

the sudden reformation in Ireland through his influence?

I have received a letter from George Combe, the bold philosopher of this age, with a present of a copy of his "Phrenological Tour," inscribed "With the respects of the author." At first glance we were somewhat disappointed in the work, his rapid step from one subject to another gave it such a desultory character; but we soon discovered marks of the philosopher's pen, and the more we read the better we liked his own views, written evidently for our improvement as well as that of his own. There is so little of mere narrative, only for selfish gratification, and so much pains taken to give valuable information, that it appears to me a work more calculated to do good than any of the kind which have preceded it.

Joseph Sturge, of Birmingham, is now in this city with John G. Whittier. My husband called to see them last evening. We quite "anticipate" — as the English say — a visit from this notable presiding officer of the "World's Convention." I shall like to look again on his pleasant smiling face. His object in stepping over is to visit Abolitionists (whether to reconcile contending parties I don't know); but "blessed are the peace-makers." Apropos. Do call at our cousin's and make friends again, forgetting hasty words uttered in the heat of party excitement. Our life is too short to lose any of it in forgetfulness of a friend. Sometimes hard feelings are continued merely from a reluctance to make the first advance in reconciliation. "To err is human; to forgive,

divine." —— has loved thee well, and I am sure
that an extended hand of returning fellowship would
be cordially met and reciprocated.   Since I have
taken such large liberties with my " brother beloved "
— both in the drawing room and in the public meeting as well as by the seaside — I feel a confidence
he will excuse this also.   One word more and I have
done.   In the temptations assailing thee in thy political career, "watch thou in all things — do the
work of an evangelist."   Thy friend,

LUCRETIA S. MOTT.

CHAPTER IX.

EXTRACTS FROM A SERMON ON "MY EXPERIENCE AS A
CLERGYMAN."

HE that hath ears to hear, let him hear."—Matt. xi. 15.

It is a great misfortune to have no ears. It is a greater calamity when one's ears are too long, and may be a great fault as well.

For in the latter case, the deafness is on the inside; in the former, it is only external. I do not suppose Jesus on that occasion imagined any of his auditors to be deaf in the ordinary meaning of that word. What he meant to imply was, I presume, that some of them had no spiritual ears, or that those interior organs were closed so that his voice, falling upon them, could make no impression of its significance. The verse from the preceding text implies, also, or seems to imply, that this was their fault or sin. For the verse says, "And if ye will, receive it." There are none so deaf as those who *will* not hear. So, on another occasion, Jesus, still appearing to connect this spiritual deafness with the principle of volition, says, "Take heed, therefore, *how* you hear."

Perhaps either passage may be taken as the equivalent of the other. . . .

Some people have a marvellous, a fatal facility of

hearing what it suits them to hear. Sometimes they hear the thing that is not said; sometimes what was said in a general or an impersonal sense, as if it was uttered in a specific, a personal one, just according to their prepossessions or prejudices. Of course it is impossible, by any linguistic skill, to make such people "hear," in the gospel sense of that little monosyllabic word. They would be likely to hear the voice of the resurrection trump as a call to do anything else, than to settle the outstanding claims against themselves.

Yet there are ministers who take infinite pains to adapt their speech to the inverted auricular organisms of such. But I never knew a minister of that sort to succeed, or who ought to have succeeded.

Of things said in an impersonal way and heard in a personal sense, I remember many instances in my own experience.

One of them I will relate. I once preached about making haste to be rich. The sermon bore, if I rightly recollect, somewhat hard upon fraudulent bankrupts. On the following day I received from a member of the church a letter nearly as long as the sermon. It was an objurgatory remonstrance against my audacity in having levelled a discourse at a private gentleman who had had the misfortune to fail, who had done me no harm, and who had been a long-paying subscriber to the support of my ministry. It was the first intimation given me of my friend's bankruptcy, which had occurred on the day before.

Of course I instantly replied to his unexpected missive; and this was the substance of my reply:

"I was not aware of your misfortune until informed thereof by your note. I do not preach to angels, and I know of no one in my society who is either good enough or bad enough to justify a minister in making him the object of a special sermon. The sermon I preached yesterday, I believed. I believe it none the less now. I regret only the feebleness with which its truths were enforced. I am bound to add, that if those truths, though not intended for your especial benefit, did yet, as you induce me to infer, meet the needs of your case, if there was in them aught 'profitable,' either 'for doctrine, for reproof, for correction,' or 'for instruction in righteousness,' I am only the more glad that it was all uttered then and there." Now of the wisdom of that reply I have nothing to say. It seemed, subsequently, to myself, somewhat brusque. But it was honest. I believed then, as I believe now, in the homely saw of that perpendicular carpenter who said, "I will hew to the line, though the chips fly in my own eyes." And I am happy to add that such frank dealing, so ingenuous an assertion of the rights of one standing in the pulpit, broke no friendship between that parishioner and his clergyman. I think the latter never preached, and the former never heard, the worse for it. . . .

And now let me say I have not selected the words of my text, because I fancy that what I have this morning to say to you is more important than other topics to which, on former occasions, I have asked your attention.

The truth is, unlike some of my clerical brethren,

I do not always find myself so happy as to be able to put my finger on a passage of scripture just suited to serve as a text for the subject I wish to speak of. I was told of one who found not only every verse of the Bible, but every letter of both Testaments, fraught with such various and large signification as to suggest to his mind innumerable subjects for solemn services. He instanced the letter S, which he observed to be the initial of the words Satan, sin, salvation, Saviour, and I know not of what others.

I have often chosen, and expect often to choose, a passage for a text, simply because it would answer. A reason no profounder than that prompted the choice of my present text.

I propose to say something of my experience as a minister, and of its antecedents.

I wish I could do so without subjecting myself to even the appearance of egotism. The experience in reference, even if it were a subject of some consequence, which it certainly is not, would be presumptuous to relate in this presence, had it no connection with matters of conceded importance. I trust it may increase your regard for the simple faith of our liberal Christianity.

Dr. Watts said he had no recollection of a time in which he did not love God. Often, however, when reading his terrific lyrical portraitures of the Deity, I have wondered how that could be. I know his case is sought to be identified, and it was deemed by himself to be identical, with that of the prophet Jeremiah (Jer. i. 5), who, we are told in the book bearing that name, was called and sanctified from the mother's

womb. But that, conceding the fancy to be a reality
and the remarkable hymnist better, even from the
start and before it, than almost all other human
creatures, should but increase wonder, since it seems
incredible that love in such a one should be the predominant feeling towards a Being who either could
not or would not rescue *all* his creatures from a doom
so horrible as that to which the overwhelming masses
of them are consigned in so many a stanza of that
popular sacred lyrist. I therefore incline to regard
those terrific portraitures as certain licenses of the
art poetic, in which even so pious an author as Dr.
Watts might have thought lawful occasionally to
indulge his muse. And I know it is believed by
many that the hope he entertained for himself, he
came, before passing to its consummation, to entertain for every son and daughter of Adam. Not that
I quite agree with Gerrit Smith, who says nobody
believes in endless punishment, or with Theodore
Parker, who says of those professing to hold the
doctrine, that "they only believe they believe it." I
think there have been, and are, persons actually believing it. The records of our mad-houses I also
think prove that fact. I believed it myself once, and
it poisoned my young life. The virus of that poison,
I sometimes fear me, has not even yet been quite ex-
pelled from my psychological system, though so many
years have elapsed since the dogma as such was ex-
pelled from my system of faith, and thrown forever
with indignation and disgust to the moles and bats of
exploded superstitions.

And I cannot say for myself in any proper sense of

the expression, that I remember no period in which I
did not love God. My boyish soul was prevented
by a frightful theology from looking up to him as a
loving Father, and rather bowed tremblingly before
him as the Almighty Sovereign of the universe.
Theodore Parker says he got entirely rid of the
damnation part of the old theology before he was
seven years old, and has had no fear of God since.
I was not so fortunate as that. Nay, I do not know
it to be desirable that any one not yet — as who of us
is? — "perfect" in love, should *be* divested of the fear
of God.

"Perfect love," we are assured, and I believe that,
"casteth out fear." And we are told that "the fear
of the Lord is the beginning of wisdom," though it
were a sad mistake to suppose, as some seem to do,
that it is also the ending thereof. No, I was not so
fortunate as that. The horrific eyeballs of that old
monster, Calvinism, glared upon me until I reached
the age of more than twice seven years. And its
ministers, I well remember, seemed to my youthful
imagination wellnigh so many incarnations of that
grim theology.

Among those whom I was accustomed to hear
preach was Dr. Emmons himself, perhaps almost the
last of the unmitigated clerical Calvinists of New
England. Their preaching, which was a fervent en-
forcement of the five points of the Assembly's shorter
catechism, which I was forced to learn by heart and
recite even at the day school, often made each particular hair of my little head stand on end. And
how often, when transfixed and writhing on those

quintuple points, and expecting my agonies to be
intensified by the sermon to come, have I been
startled by the austere parson's terrible opening of
the Sunday service. For often it was opened in this
wise : "Let us sing, to the praise and glory of God,
the second hymn of the second book, common metre."

> "My thoughts on awful subjects roll,
> Damnation and the dead;
> What horrors seize the guilty soul
> Upon a dying bed!
>
> Lingering about these mortal shores,
> She makes a long delay;
> Till, like a flood with rapid force,
> Death sweeps the wretch away.
>
> Then, swift and dreadful she descends
> Down to the fiery coast;
> Amongst abominable fiends,
> Herself a frightful ghost.
>
> There endless crowds of sinners lie,
> And darkness makes their chains;
> Tortured with keen despair, they cry,
> Yet wait for fiercer pains.
>
> Not all their anguish and their blood
> For their old guilt atones;
> Nor the compassion of a God
> Shall hearken to their groans."

And then, in closing the service of the sanctuary,
after a sermon on the fewness of those to be saved,
and portraying "God's fiery indignation" against the
non-elect, we were almost sure to be called on to
join in singing a "spiritual song" such as the following : —

" Behold the aged sinner goes,
    Laden with guilt and heavy woes,
    Down to the regions of the dead,
    With endless curses on his head.

For in the deep where darkness dwells,
    The land of horror and despair,
    Justice has built a dismal hell,
    And laid her stores of vengeance there.

Eternal plagues and heavy chains,
    Tormenting racks and fiery coals,
    And darts, inflict immortal pains,
    Dyed in the blood of damned souls.

There Satan the first sinner lies,
    And roars, and bites his iron bands:
    In vain the rebel strives to rise,
    Crushed with the weight of both thy hands."

EXTRACTS FROM A SERMON ON JOHN BROWN, THE MARTYR.

" Remember them that are in bonds, as bound with them." (Heb. xiii. 8.)

" Undo the heavy burdens; break every yoke, and let the oppressed go free."

" All things whatsoever ye would that men should do to you, do ye even so to them; for this is the law and the prophets." (Matt. vii. 12.)

" We hold these truths to be self-evident, that all men are created equal; that they are endowed by their Creator with certain inalienable rights; that among these are life, liberty, and the pursuit of happiness; that, to secure these rights, governments are instituted among men, deriving their just powers from the consent of the governed." (" A declaration by the representatives of the United States of America, in Congress assembled," July 4, 1776.)

"If I had interfered, in behalf of the rich, the powerful, the intelligent, the so-called great, or any of their friends, parents, wives or children, it would all have been right. No man in this country would have thought it a crime. But I believe that to have interfered as I have done for the despised poor, I have done no wrong, but right." (John Brown, before the mock court that murdered him.)

My subject is John Brown, the Martyr; the cause of his martyrdom; and what has come of it. On the last Sunday I spoke of honesty. To-day I wish we may all, the auditors not less than the speaker, exercise a little of that precious virtue. If that shall be done, and a little intelligence and a little reflection should be mingled with the exercise, there will be found, I trust, little difference of opinion among us in regard to any conclusions sought to be reached, excepting, perhaps, in the case of some — if any such are present — who hold to the doctrine of non-resistance.

I do not hold to that doctrine. I cherish, however, a peculiar respect for those who do; those who, like my friend Mrs. Child, consistently hold it, and therefore, while staying their hands, hold their tongues also from smiting with hard words, and from crying out to the wrong-doer, "Vengeance is mine, I will repay, saith the Lord;" as if God were less forbearing, more vindictive, than they. There is no scorpion that stings more than a sharp tongue. David, who had so often felt and used that instrument,

pronounced it "a sharp sword." Solomon tells us
that "death and life are in the power of the tongue."
And he who does not dread the tongue of a termagant more than both her fists, has had an experience
more fortunate than that of either "the wise man" or
the psalmist. I have, therefore, been long of the
opinion that it is a capital defect in the common law
to make a blow of the fist a greater provocation than
one from the tongue.

I also am for peace. But it must be based on
justice. I also can shout the benediction "of the
angel," and "a multitude of the heavenly host," as
reported by Luke; only I must give it in the rendering of Kossuth and our Catholic friends, "Glory to
God in the highest, and, on earth, peace to men of
good-will." No others are or can be entitled to
peace; for "there is no peace to the wicked, saith
my God." In other words, and to close this reference to our non-resistant friends, I am in agreement
with old Barnveldt, the martyr, who exclaimed, "Let
us have peace if possible, but justice at any rate."

Do not take the observations which have been
made as meant to vindicate my text. I should be
either base or foolish if I sought to justify that in a
country whose people in the proportion of perhaps
ten thousand to one, profess to accept the Declaration
of Independence, and an equal proportion of whose
professing Christians, whatever their faith in "the
sword of the Lord," we all know have quite as much
in that "of Gideon." Indeed, American Christians
who profess to have repudiated the Old Testament,
and American patriots who profess to have repu-

diated the Declaration, are almost as rare as white blackbirds.

And that fact makes me impatient with those clergymen who have been giving us homilies on loving slaveholders, while remembering "them that are in bonds, as bound with them." Such homilies, to say the least of them, are ill-timed. They have the effect of speeches made to mobs by cowardly magistrates, about the impudence, the "incendiary language," of the persons mobbed, when all that was clearly needed was grape for the mobocrats, not "sermons and soda-water" for their victims. You have all read of the Boston massacre. Suppose the pastors of Warren, Otis, Adams and Hancock had set themselves to lecturing "the friends of freedom" on that occasion about the importance of throwing the arms of their charity around the assassins while sympathizing with the slain : what would such patriots have said of such preaching? Did that most patient man, Job, lack due sympathy for oppressors? What clergyman says he did? Yet, you will not have forgotten, "the man of Uz" claims it as a thing most creditable to his "philanthropy" that he "brake the jaws of the wicked, and delivered the spoil out of his mouth." I know the command is, "Love your enemies." But in what sense? In the sense of incurring the sin of the priests of Israel, denounced by the Almighty God for having "put no difference between the holy and profane," and "shown" none "between the unclean and the clean"? I trow not. We know that all American patriots, and, with exceptions almost too few to merit even this reference, all Americans Christians, see in the injunction "Love your enemies," nothing inconsistent with shooting them, especially when they happened to be Englishmen levying threepence a pound on the tea of our good grandmothers. And how few of either see in that commandment aught incompatible with putting bullets and bayonets through the brains and hearts of the Mexicans, whose enmity consisted in resisting the dismemberment of their government, and the pollution of their free soil with the curse of slavery! How few among us all feel that there has been any lack of love for even our Indian enemies, made such only by our robbery of their lands, and our banishment of them from the graves of their fathers! Happy are the people who condemn not themselves in those things which they allow!

> "O wad some power the giftie gie us
> To see oursels as others see us!
> It wad frae monie a blunder free us
>   An' foolish notion;
> What airs in dress an' gait wad leave us,
>   And ev'n devotion!"

Of John Brown I have nothing new to tell you, nothing of which the substance, at least, has not been already given to the public.

He believed in God. His character was Cromwellian, but more transparent and honest. It shone out on all occasions, principally before the court. His "raid" was not "a failure." And I do not say that only because I believe, with Byron, that —

> "Freedom's battle, once begun,
> Bequeathed from bleeding sire to son,
> Though baffled oft, is ever won."

Neither do I say it only because, as Bryant has it —

"Truth crushed to earth will rise again;
The eternal years of God are hers."

I say it because I believe it is one of those defeats which are in themselves "victories;" because I believe that a few more such would bring down the old bastille of slavery, as surely as the less horrible one in France fell beneath the blows of the revolutionists of '89.

I said that John Brown had faith in God. The man who has that, believes likewise in principles. With the heart, man believeth unto salvation. He believed with the heart, with his whole heart; and with a heart so large as his, how mighty must have been his faith! It was a faith which removes mountains, and shakes half a continent. The faith of most men in God, in truth, in immortality, is a thing merely of the head, and therefore, at the most, little else than a "great perhaps." Principles are jeered at. Those of the Declaration were stigmatized by the greatest advocate America has produced, as "glittering generalities." The golden rule is read, "Do unto others as others do unto you;" and the practical construction is often worse.

But with John Brown, this rule, and that Declaration, meant what they say. The principles of either pulsated in every throb of his big heart. In the one, he recognized what I remember John C. Spencer once pronounced it, "the paramount law of this nation;" in the other, the supreme cosmopolitan law of the Christian faith. And the resolute, persistent, never-yielding resolve to do what in him lay, or rather the actual doing of what in him lay, to resolve both to practice, — that was John Brown's grandest characteristic. That it was which made him loom above the herd of men usually called great, as Chimborazo towers above the molehill. And for that it was that, forty-nine hours ago, Virginia hanged him like a dog. And so, oh, "chivalrous Virginians," denizens of "the old Dominion," dwellers in the land which gave Washington his birth, and his bones a resting-place, if the bones of such a man can longer repose beneath its surface, you have at once made those vaunting expressions as eternally ridiculous as infamous, and the gallows as certainly an emblem of honor as the crucifixion of Jesus by the less degenerate Romans transformed the ignominious cross into a symbol of glory. "Thanks be to God, who giveth us the victory," the manliness of the one, no more than that of the other, suffered any diminution by the mode of his emancipation into the eternal life!

And now our —

> "Duncan is in his grave;
> After life's fitful fever he sleeps well;
> Treason has done his worst: Nor steel, nor poison,
> Malice domestic, foreign levy, nothing
> Can touch him further."

And no doubt those fools of the Virginian chivalry think *that* is an end of him; that they have killed Duncan himself.

But whoso has faith in the world of realities, knows they have only raised him to a higher life; given him a passport to a field of more efficient action, even against the special iniquity which sent him to Virginia, to the scaffold, and to the world of causes.

> " Besides, this Duncan
> Hath borne his faculties so meek, hath been
> So clear in his great office, that his virtues
> Will plead like angels, trumpet-tongued, against
> The deep damnation of his taking off.
> And pity, like a naked new-born babe,
> Striding the blast, or Heav'n's cherubim horsed
> Upon the sightless couriers of the air,
> Shall blow the horrid deed in every eye,
> That tears shall drown the wind."

An effort, you know, was made to prove Brown a victim of insanity. I cannot say I am sorry it did not succeed. I do not know that it would have been pleasant to reflect that we owed to a lunatic what seems the noblest exhibition of courage, energy, honesty, faith in ideas, reverence for God and devotion to man, even leaving out the point of sagacity, which the age has yet witnessed. If Brown *was* mad, there was a terrible "method in his madness." But I see neither in the invasion of Virginia nor in the affidavits taken to prove him mad, *proof* that he was so. The former, judging it by the results, was a very sensible movement, in comparison of Louis Napoleon's first invasion of France. Louis Napoleon, and some score of tatterdemalions accompanying him, were caught up and placed in the calaboose within fifteen minutes after landing at Boulogne. John Brown kept the whole State of Virginia at bay some forty-eight hours, and was finally conquered, not by " the Old Dominion," but by a company of marines employed and chiefly paid by the people of what we call the free States. Wise for once indicated his patronymic by saying he would rather his right arm were slashed off up to the shoulder, than that conquest should not have been made by the citizens of his own State. Louis Napoleon did not frighten a solitary Frenchman. John Brown frightened the Virginians out of all the wit that he found in them.

No competent judges dispute that Brown's invasion was an efficient blow at the slave power. I see, or think I see, it has weakened that power. Of course I cannot find in his sagacity to *foresee* that such would be the effect of it, any proof of insanity. . .

Remember, the estimate which I have presented of this new recruit of "the noble army of martyrs" is based not on any mere views of my own, but on the authority, as I might say, of our two bibles, the scriptures of the Old and New Testaments and the Declaration of American Independence.

In the name of what logical force God has lodged in this brain of mine, I do most solemnly affirm that unless both those bibles, or at least so much of them as forms my text, ought to be burned, I have not said a syllable too much in praise of John Brown.

The cause of this martyrdom, I now need hardly say, is slavery. If a conspiracy of pirates were to set up a powder-magazine in our village, and a spark from some chimney were to explode it, causing a general conflagration, you would all pronounce the real cause of the fire to be, not in the embers of our hearth-stones, but in that depot of saltpetre. The explosion of the powder-house might indeed be not the only cause of the conflagration. If any among us had possessed the power to abolish the nuisance before the spark had fallen upon it, and refused to exercise that power, those so refusing might be justly enough deemed *another* cause of the fire. . . .

What has come, and may come, of the doings of this martyr we know of course only in part. Of this we are certain : he has done for the Virginians what conscience ought long since to have done for them ; he has made cowards of them all, and some of them are not mad, only because it requires *some* mind as a condition precedent of insanity. He also has done more, perhaps, than any thousand others to call attention to slavery. That is an inestimable service to the cause of freedom. For slavery, like vice, or rather because comprehending all vice,

> — "is a monster of so frightful mien,
> That to be hated needs but to be seen."

EXTRACTS FROM A SERMON ON WOMAN'S RIGHTS.

"There is neither Jew nor Greek, there is neither bond nor free, there is neither male nor female : for ye are all one in Christ Jesus " (Gal. iii. 28).

I shall speak to you this morning of "woman's rights." I confess, though, that I should have preferred for my subject some other designation. For the expression "woman's rights" implies a certain duality, or rather a sort of antagonism, which I do not myself recognize. "Male" and "female," as used in my text, "man" and "woman," as popularly employed, are but species of the same genus, correlative parts of a common whole ; and what, in respect of essential rights, may be predicated of either, that, it appears to me, is alike predicable of the other.

I have, too, a notion that it takes two, male and

female, to constitute an entire human being, just as certainly as both sexes are required to form a race of such beings. So, in correspondence with the idea now hinted at, the word "man" in our Bible is translated sometimes from one and sometimes from the other of two different words, which, alike in the Hebrew, the Greek and the Latin language, designate an important distinction; I mean that of the sexes, which, from the imperfectness of our tongue, can be expressed, in the latter only by a periphrasis or circumlocution.

But all that is in allusion, somewhat darkly it may be fancied, to the interior essence, or at least to one of the higher aspects, of an institution which it is no part of my present purpose to discuss. Franklin, were he less coarsely utilitarian, might be supposed to have had the same thing in his mind when he spoke of the unmarried person as little better than the odd half of a pair of scissors, which might indeed serve to scrape a trencher, but not for any very noble function.

I might have named my subject, borrowing the title which has been employed by I know not how many clergymen and others, "the appropriate sphere of woman." But it has always seemed to me, at least it has so seemed ever since, by observation, reflection and contact with the world, the professional starch was taken out of me — to be a little ridiculous in any man, whether a clergyman or a layman, to undertake to mark out the boundaries of that sphere, or show precisely, what is fit or not fitting, for the other half of humanity.

The ridiculousness of such a proceeding would perhaps appear even to those who so often embark in it, if women were to set about defining "the appropriate sphere of man." The women in such a case would doubtless be told to mind their own business. But in this, as in other matters, I hold by the old saw, "It is a poor rule that won't work both ways." My wife, I concede, nay, affirm, has just as good a right to determine the length of my beard — which in point of fact, I should, if pushed be obliged to confess she has done — as I have to fix the diameter of her crinoline. Nay, that comparison hardly does justice to the conception; since it is quite conceivable that either party, in such a case, might have grounds for protesting, the one against the hirsute, the other against the dress appendage, each as an invasion of the other's personal freedom.

I have used the expression "woman's rights," in naming my subject, because it has come to be a popular one, however inappropriate, and is used to designate a party, or rather a growing number of people, as well in this country as in others, who claim for women an equality with men. . . .

I do not profess to find the equality of the sexes *explicitly* taught in the Bible, even in the New Testament part of it. I claim only that the doctrine is deducible from the spirit of its teachings; at the same time conceding that "the letter," or much of it, seems to inculcate the opposite opinion. . . .

It nevertheless appears that women, even in those days and under that dark dispensation, were not all mere menials. For some of them rose to be teachers, leaders, even deliverers of their nation. None were indeed admitted to the Jewish priesthood, but some were recognized as prophets, an office more clearly correspondent than that of priests to the function of modern clergymen. Thus Huldah is spoken of as a prophetess dwelling at the college in Jerusalem; Anna as another living in the temple; Deborah as both a prophetess and a judge; and Miriam, Aaron's sister, as a prophetess who led the procession, the songs and the dances over the great "John Brown raid" in Egypt, which, under the lead of Moses, resulted in running off a nation of slaves, and burying their piratical pursuers in the closing waters of the Red Sea, typical, it may have been, of the doom which awaits the American Pharaohs.

And then there were among the Jews women who won a yet greater conspicuity, a wider or at least a more rapturous applause by their deeds of daring. There were among them veritable Charlotte Cordays, though I remember no Joans of Arc. Such were Judith and Jael, whose exploits, whether for courage or for cunning, have not been surpassed by any celebrated by Cooper in his romances of our Indian braves, while they indicated an amount of patriotism sufficient to set up a thousand populations of American Union-savers.

Judith saved from utter destruction the union of Israel, and Israel itself, by decapitating Holofernes with his own "fanchion." And "then," so the history reads, "Joachim the high priest, and the ancients of the children of Israel that dwelt in Jerusalem, came to behold the good things that God had showed to Israel, and to see Judith, and to salute her. And when they came unto her, they blessed her with one accord, and said unto her, 'thou art the exaltation of Jerusalem, thou art the great rejoicing of our nation : thou hast done all these things by thy hand : thou hast done much good to Israel, and God is pleased therewith : blessed be thou of the almighty God forevermore.' And all the people said, so be it."

And Jael's exploit, accompanied by like demonstrations of rejoicing, was, you know, performed by her upon Sisera, though, it must be confessed, the courage in either case would have been more admirable but for the violation of the rights of hospitality and trickery resorted to by those courageous, cunning women.

But, whatever superiority or excellence, whether of courage, of judicial wisdom, of prophetic vision, or of whatever other admirable quality the Jewish women may have exhibited, it is plain that such qualities never availed to win for their sex any recognition of its equality with the other. Perhaps it was creditable to so stiff-necked a people, as their own prophets so often called the Jews, that they should have consented, now and then, to be saved by a woman. There have been men who would rather give up the ghost than be saved by such an instrumentality. At any rate, I remember to have read in Greek or Roman history of a man who, having been conquered by one of the opposite sex, killed himself; and it is certain that many a man has died of failing to conquer a woman.

The beau-ideal of a woman, as furnished by the

author of the Book of Proverbs, in the 31st chapter
of that book, is that of a hard-working, painstaking,
thrifty, pious housewife, who, in the words of that
author, "looketh well to the ways of her household,
and eateth not the bread of idleness;" who, by her
wit, prudence, handicraft, unintermitting industry,
tact and skill in bargaining, provides so liberally for
all the inmates of her establishment, without forgetting the claims of poor outsiders, that "the heart of
her husband" "doth safely trust in her, so that he
hath no need of spoil," and "is known in the gates
when he sitteth among the elders of the land." That
is the ideal woman of the author of the Book of
Proverbs, commonly supposed to have been Solomon, whom the catechism of my boyhood bade me
call the wise man.

He names her a "virtuous woman." I think if his
own "seven hundred wives" were all of that sort,
cavillers need go no further to find how he got the
means to build even so magnificent a temple as that
of Jerusalem.

And if the women of these days were but so many
"more of the same sort," I have no doubt there would
be a great rush among them for wives, especially by
the lame, the lazy, and every purseless fellow whose
ambition it is to be "known in the gates."

I am almost ashamed to say *that* is not *my* beau-
ideal.

I find in the reported teachings of *Jesus* nothing
which, in either its letter or its spirit, can be fairly
quoted against the broadest claims of the woman's-
rights party. . . . .

CHAPTER X.

EXTRACTS FROM A LECTURE ON HUMBUG.

MOST people are best pleased with what they least need; and most popular lecturers consult rather the wishes than the wants of their hearers. Therefore I am not an ardent admirer of "popular lectures." Yet if a subject were popular in proportion as it concerns us, mine should have a popularity unsurpassed; for it is "Humbug," and therefore one in which we are all interested, either as victims or as agents.

I distinguish two kinds of humbug: the impersonal and personal. My remarks, now, will be devoted to the former. There is a vein of humbug running through wellnigh all that passes for history.

Sir Robert Walpole, when his son proposed to read to him from "a volume of history," said he would not hear it, for he knew "it must be false." Another Englishman, Bolingbroke, tells us, "History is philosophy teaching by examples." And so it is, if only the "examples" are made sure of. But to be certain of his examples, of his facts, that is precisely the historian's great difficulty. Said Dr. Johnson, "The hardest thing in the world, sir, is to get possession of a fact." Perhaps it is only less difficult to state one. And I suppose it is therefore, chiefly, that so much that is called history were better named fiction, whether treating of persons, of parties, of sects or of nations.

The person occupying the most space in modern history is Napoleon Bonaparte. His "Life," by Sir Walter Scott, a Frenchman pronounced the greatest of that author's romances. I heard O'Connell say, " Wellington won the battle of Waterloo by accident." The remark might be justified by citations from scores of historical writers, though Scott ascribes "the Man of Destiny's " overthrow to "the Iron Duke's " adroit generalship, and the indomitable energy of British soldiers.

Was Napoleon a great man? Carlyle says, " Napoleon does by no means seem to me as great a man as Cromwell." And Channing in the paper which won him his trans-Atlantic reputation, dividing greatness into three orders, assigns Napoleon to the lowest, and says he was not pre-eminent in that. Emerson concedes that "he was a great scamp." The Rev. John S. C. Abbott says, "He was the greatest of mankind."

Was he — if I may put the question without raising a laugh — also a godly man? Baupet, many years near the Emperor's person, says, "He had so much scepticism as to question whether Jesus Christ ever existed ! " Channing was shocked by his impiety. But Abbott says, "The religious element predominated in the bosom of Napoleon."

I do not find, after reading some half a hundred volumes about him, if Napoleon, before divorcing Josephine, had lost his love for that accomplished woman.

The Duchess d'Abrantes says he had. But since that fascinating woman fancied herself to be an object of the Emperor's special fondness, it may safely be concluded she was a little biased in the premises. One thing is certain, and that is, when Napoleon abandoned Josephine, Fortune forgetting her fickleness, abandoned the Emperor. "No son of his," but what a Nemesis! a grandson of the discarded Empress "succeeding." One other thing is equally certain. All the *women* who have sat on this question, concur in the verdict, "Served him right!"

Take another case, — that of an extraordinary Frenchman; for Napoleon was not a Frenchman. "He was," as Goldwin Smith in his last book so significantly says, "he was a Corsican." If Robespierre — for that is the notable Frenchman alluded to — was not a wolf in fierceness, a tiger in cruelty, a leopard in treachery, an ass in stupidity, then nearly all history, in so far as it treats of the Deputy of Arras, is fraught with humbug.

Yet Lamartine in his better days proclaimed him "the Luther of politics," "the philosopher of the Revolution." Others, besides deeming him able and eloquent, praise his disinterestedness, his patriotism, his philanthropy; while the title so proudly claimed for him by his friends, that of "the incorruptible," seems admitted by all to have been merited; though the "Edinburgh Review" once said, "he was incorruptible, not because he was above bribery, but because, like certain animals, he was below it."

English history abounds in similar discrepancies. According to some of its writers, there never was a more vulgar brutal rebel than Wat Tyler. An American dining with the London Fishmongers' Society, complimented that body on its honor in having enrolled among its members "the man who slew Wat Tyler." That American was minister of the United States at the Court of St. James, and had helped make John Tyler an American President.

Punch, taking in an extra quantity of lemon, was particularly pungent on the occasion of such an exhibition of himself by an ambassador of the sole great democracy of earth. For it knew that, according to sharp explorers of English history, the crime of Wat Tyler consisted in his practical sympathy with human rights. Southey before turning Tory had made that brawny blacksmith the hero of his truest poem. The difference between Wat Tyler and John Tyler was this simply: the one was an honest Democrat, not unlike our John Brown; he and his brother-peasants rising to protect themselves from robbery, their wives and daughters from outrage, by the brutal myrmidons of a royal tyrant. The other was a humbug Democrat, because a Slaveocrat, and at the last yet logically (because still in the interest of the "sum of all villanies," as the sainted John Wesley called American slavery) a traitor to a government which his own chiefs, Davis and Stephens, had pronounced the best the world ever knew.

And if Macaulay and others were not wrong, then Bacon was "the wisest, brightest, meanest of mankind." But if we may believe others, especially Montagu, certainly one of the ablest, and, for aught I can see, also one of the fairest of the great chancellor's biographers, Bacon's peculiar crime consisted in consenting to sacrifice himself rather than seem ungrateful to James and Buckingham. He indeed confessed to have accepted presents, but denied that they ever influenced his decisions; denied that he could be fairly accused of aught worse than selling justice; protesting strenuously that he "never sold injustice;" and we all know that in this nineteenth century, people seeking justice in the courts are only too glad if not forced to pay for injustice.

What a canting hypocrite, what an ambitious, cruel usurper, was Oliver Cromwell, if we may take the asseverations of most British historians, or even of our own Bancroft! Yet what a modest, straight-forward, God-fearing man, what a devout worshipper of eternal justice, what an earnest friend of the race, was that same Oliver Cromwell, if we may accept the statements of his foreign secretary, the immortal Milton, and in later times of Carlyle and others!

The same holds of American history. Bancroft praises William Penn, his ability, his statesmanship, his Christian character.

But Macaulay writes almost contemptuously of both the head and the heart of that famous Quaker; says he was rather a weak, vain man, that he "did not scruple to become a broker of a peculiarly discredit-able kind, and to use a bishopric as a bait to tempt a divine to perjury."

And in what historian do we find a lifelike por-trait of Washington? One of his finest traits is not touched by the accomplished and lamented Everett. I allude to Washington's abhorrence of slavery, his frequent avowal of an earnest wish to see it abolished, and his readiness to vote for its abolition. It is difficult to say if the father of our country, as he appears in most histories, is not rather a myth than a real personage. They leave one in doubt if Washington ever laughed, if he ever got angry, or, as an Englishman said he would give ten pounds to know — if he ever swore.

But I am not ashamed to confess to a feeling of satisfaction in finding that the great Washington was "of like passions with you." Once when told of a personal slander, he smote the table with a vehemence that made the cups and saucers dance a "saraband." When, at Harlem, the Connecticut troops ran away, exposing his person "to capture within eighty paces of the enemy" (Hildreth's History United States, 111, 152, September 15, 1776; Irving's Life of Washington), dashing his hat upon the ground and snapping his pistols at the scampering cowards, he cried out, "Are these the troops with which I am expected to defend America?" And when at Monmouth he met Lee retreating, he is reported to have sworn "like a trooper." What would the great patriot have done if he had lived to witness the treason of that general's descendant, Robert Lee?

I confess also to some satisfaction in Lord Mahon's rebuke of our own Sparks for the latter's euphemistic modifications of the diction of Washington's familiar letters, as if it were an "improvement" of Washington to make him eternally walk a crack! In one of those letters, Washington had spoken of the "scandalous conduct," the "dirty, mercenary spirit," of certain Connecticut troops. Sparks omits those epithets.

In another, Washington, with a delightful familiarity bringing him nearer to the hearts of us all, calls his friend Putnam "Old Put." The dainty Sparks knocks that out too, and substitutes " General Putnam."

Passing from persons to parties, what antipodal estimates are given of the old Federal and Democratic parties in the representative volumes of Sullivan and Ingersoll !

According to the one, the Hartford Convention was a noble band of patriots ; according to the other, an atrocious conspiracy of traitors. If the latter and his class were neither fools nor knaves, John Adams and his partisans of the Federal party passed the " Sedition law," to restrain, not the license, but the liberty of the press. The stock in trade of a great political party for half a century was to identify all opponents with that same Sedition law, and the elder Adams, though I find the latter was personally opposed to the enactment. But what, after all, was the principle of that much-execrated statute ? It was simply that no one has a right nor should be suffered with impunity to libel high public functionaries, and so cripple their power to serve the people. It prohibited no one from publishing the truth of men in place. On the contrary, if one could prove the truth of what he had uttered, that by the statute itself was held to be a sufficient legal defence. And what good citizen speaking for himself either could, would or should deprecate such a law as that ?

I undertake to assert that such a citizen so speaking would no more deprecate such a law than he would fly in the face of the ninth commandment. But let me not be misunderstood. I am not deprecating attacks on sham personages, whether public or private. To strip the sheep's clothing from the wolf, the peacock's plumage from the daw, the lion's skin from the ass, this, I hold, may well be, nay often is, "acceptable unto God," and ought always to be welcomed by the people.

And so of sects. What Catholic historian gives us a reliable account of Protestantism? In what Protestant author have we such an account of Catholicity? What is oftener imputed to the latter than that it persecuted Galileo for maintaining the rotary motion of the earth? Yet we have profound students of history who resent the imputation as a slander.

They, of course, do not deny that Galileo was brought before the Inquisition. But they allege that he was so arraigned because, and only because, he contumaciously endeavored to support his scientific opinions by the Bible, the Catholic Church claiming to be the authorized interpreter of that volume, and Galileo professing himself to be a faithful son of that church.

Then, as if to compound for that aspersion, if, as I believe, it *is* an aspersion of Catholics, we are told by some historians, Bancroft among them, that the Catholics of Maryland were the first in this country to secure by law the right of religious freedom.

Others award that honor to the Puritans, and yet others to the Quakers. But it belongs to none of

them. To land the Maryland Romanists as pro-
tectors of religious liberty is much as if one should
praise them as the special friends of the poor because
in their Bill of Rights they gravely asserted that
"paupers ought not to be assessed for the support of
government." They did as little for freedom of
conscience as they dared. They could not have done
less and saved their own. Besides, under their rule,
even so good a Christian as George Bancroft might
have been punished with "death" and "forfeiture of
lands and goods." Even William Penn's government
trampled on the Jews' conscience. As to the Puritans, our New England Puritans, they were an
honest people. Therefore they affected no friendship
for religious freedom excepting for themselves. And
therefore they are not to be accused of inconsistency
because they hanged Quakers and banished Roger
Williams. But as "the artist worked better than he
knew," so did our Puritans; for the banishment of
Roger Williams led to what Hildreth, our most
reliable historian as it seems to me, calls "the first
formal and legal establishment of religious liberty,
whether in America or Europe."

Of historic discrepancies in regard to nations we
have a remarkable example in the case of the Hay-
tiens.

They are still commonly reported to have won
their freedom by "cutting their masters' throats."
But historical students know it was obtained legally
and peacefully. If subsequently they flew to arms,
giving better than they got, that was to vindicate

their liberty against the atrocious attempt of Napoleon to re-enslave them.

And suppose one wishing to get some idea of the characteristics of the Russian people were to consult the Marquis De Castine's work. What would he find? He would find the learned author declaring that the Russians are a nation of thieves, that they are thieves on principle, that they practise as many kinds of theft as there are orders of society.

But shall we give up our faith in history because of the shams pervading it? I doubt if even Walpole before he broke down in politics had *no* faith in history.

We may easily suppose his case analogous to that of the woman whose horse ran away with her down the hill. "Her faith in Providence did not give out until the breeching broke." People do not lose their faith in money because bogus bills are mixed with the national currency. The legitimate effect of perceiving shams in history is to sharpen the student's optics, to extend the range of his reading, to make him try the historians, even as Paul bids us "try the spirits," an admonition too little heeded in those days, I fear.

EXTRACT FROM A LECTURE ON EDUCATION RELATING TO CLASSICAL STUDIES.

Too much, or rather too general, attention is given to the classics. Says the late Sidney Smith, "A young Englishman goes to school at six or seven years of age, and he remains in a course of education till twenty-three or twenty-four years old. In all this time his sole and exclusive occupation is learning

Latin and Greek, — he has scarcely a notion that there is any other kind of excellence, — and the great system of facts with which he is most perfectly acquainted are the intrigues of the heathen gods. It is no uncommon thing to meet with English gentlemen whom, but for their gray hairs and wrinkles, we might easily mistake for school-boys. Their talk is of Latin verses; and it is quite clear, if men's ages are to be dated from the state of their mental progress, that such men are eighteen years of age and not a day older.

"Look at all the terms of applause of the public! A learned man! a scholar! a man of erudition! Upon whom are these epithets of approbation bestowed? Are they given to men acquainted with the science of government? — thoroughly masters of the geographical and commercial relations of Europe? — to men who know the properties of bodies and their action upon each other? No! this is not learning. It is chemistry, or political economy — not learning." And a living poet says, —

"One while the fever is to learn what none will be wiser for knowing,
Exploded errors in extinct tongues, and occasions for their use are small;
And the bright morning of life, for years of misspent time,
Wasted in following sounds, hath tracked up little sense,
Till at noon a man is thrown upon the world with a mind expert in trifles,
Having yet everything to learn that can make him good or useful.
The curious spirit of youth is crammed with unwholesome garbage,
While starving for the mother's milk the breasts of nature yield;

And high-colored fables of depravity lure with their classic
    varnish,
While truth is holding out in vain her mirror much despised."

But this grave joke of the classics has not been
carried quite so far with us. I know not that even
the faculty and corporation of Yale would push it to
this extent. If, as Talleyrand once said, "words *are*
things," they are not those of heathen Greece, nor of
heathen Rome. The author of that smart saying
himself would not have pretended it.

Dr. Spurzheim, who sometimes wrote in Latin as
well as lectured in three or four of the living languages, complained, when examined for admission into
the London College of Surgeons, of being asked if
he knew Latin. He thought it enough if he were
acquainted with the science he proposed to practise,
and remarked that he anticipated no occasion for
talking to his patients in Latin. The acquisition of
one new idea is of more value than that of twenty
new names for an old one.

There was wisdom, therefore, in the reply of Dr.
Franklin when asked why he did not study the classics. He found his own language adequate to the
expression of the ideas he had, and chose to occupy
his time in teaching those and learning new ones.
There *was* a time when such a reply would have been
foolishness. For there was a time when those languages, with the Hebrew, embodied the knowledge
of civilization. But that time has long since passed;
and now, probably, there is not in any of those languages one important idea but may be found in
Franklin's vernacular. And what in this respect was

true in that philosopher's day is pre-eminently so at this.

But what are the great arguments for the study of the classics? For it might be deemed hardly respectful in me to pass them by without a word, after what I have said. One is, that the study disciplines, strengthens the mind, fitting it for profound inquiry and deep reflection. I admit that it does so. Such, also, was the effect of studying alchemy.

It is then scarcely a sufficient recommendation of a study, that it invigorates the mind. It should do more. It should put knowledge into it at the same time; knowledge that would avail somewhat in the affairs of this working world. But, says President Everett, instituting an ingenious comparison of mental and physical gymnastics, "It never was required of a man who wished to exercise his limbs and stir his blood, to place himself on a treadmill which gives motion to some useful machinery."

But why not? The fact, that it *has not* been, is not quite a conclusive reason that it *should not* be so required of a man. If all the advantages a man seeks in physical gymnastics could be equally well obtained by placing "himself on a treadmill which gives motion to some useful machinery," he *ought* to mount the mill; if a benevolent man, he would *do* so; if a minor, he should, perhaps, be *made* to do so, if need were. But the cases are not parallel. The treadmill would not answer the purpose sought in physical gymnastics. But the mental discipline alleged to be given by the study of languages may be as well given by other studies; studies which would at the same time impress the mind with more valuable ideas for subsequent use. So that President Everett's conclusion, "that in this respect, the gymnastics of the mind [meaning its exercise in lingual studies] stand on as good a footing as those of the body," is not at all warranted.

But, in truth, the premise itself of this whole argument is mainly a groundless assumption. For the whole intellect is not employed in the study of languages. Only a small portion of its faculties are employed in that study, and the principal of these are very inferior faculties, found often more powerful in semi-idiots, than in some men of gigantic minds.

It is the verbal memory chiefly that is exercised by lingual studies. I once met a man who, it was said, could recite from memory the whole Bible. I satisfied myself he could do so. It would seem that a word had never fallen upon his auditory apparatus without fixing itself indelibly in the memory. Yet this was a very imbecile man. He had almost no conception of the significance of the words he recited. "I don't," said he to me, "read anything but the Scriptures, psalm-book and almenick; for if I git anything in my head, I can never git it out agin, and am afeared I might git something bad in it." There is, or was some years ago, in Liverpool, a Mr. Jones who evinced a similar familiarity with the classics. These this Englishman had at his tongue's end, though scarcely competent to put two ideas together and infer from them a third one.

In both, we have a practical illustration of that

line of Shakspeare's, "The fool hath planted in his memory an army of good words." I do not know whether Sir Hudibras, —

> " Whose tongue ran on the more,
> The less of weight it bore,
> And, with its everlasting clack,
> Set all men's ears upon the rack," —

was, or was not, a linguist. But I know he *might* have been one. Even the Marquis Moscati, who, chiefly amid the bustle of camps, — for, joining the standard of Napoleon at an early age, he followed him in all his campaigns, — acquired an acquaintance with thirty-six languages, and became a master of twenty of them, the Latin, Hebrew and Greek being among the latter, was not, I believe, remarkable for the strength of his general intellect, which, by the argument I am considering, should have been colossal. How it may be with that other Italian who could speak fifty-two and read sixty-four languages, I know not; but as Rome does not often put a cardinal's hat on a mere head full of words, Mezzofanti's was doubtless a respectable brain.

And my friend "the learned blacksmith," who has mastered some three dozen of languages, is considered more distinguished by largeness of heart than by greatness of intellect; though I would by no means intimate that the latter is not superior to most men's. On the other hand, some of the mightiest minds have had no aptitude for the study of words, have abandoned it in despair.

A Washington in statesmanship, a Napoleon in

arms, a Franklin in philosophy, a Marshall in juris-
prudence, a Fielding in romance, a Henry in eloquence, and "one Will Shakspeare" in poetry, de-
monstrate the possibility of some considerable success in the higher departments of mental exertion,
with the smallest possible knowledge of the defunct
tongues of those old Greeks and Romans.   Should it
be said that no regard has been paid in these remarks
to the philosophy of those tongues which certainly
demands the exertion of the higher faculties, the reply would be, that the philosophy of all languages is
the same, and may, of course, be studied as well in
one's vernacular as elsewhere.

Another argument for the study of the classics is,
that it is necessary to a thorough knowledge and skilful use of our own language, which is in a measure
derived from the Greek and Latin.   The principle of
this argument would require also the study of I know
not how many other languages from which ours has
borrowed words.   Why not, then, be a little logical,
and insist that nobody can know and write the Queen's
English who has not mastered every other language
from which it has derived a syllable?   But I would
beg to be informed if this Queen's English, this native tongue, — shall I be pardoned for saying it? — of
the greatest people on the surface of the earth, — a
language destined, perhaps, to be the vernacular of
the globe, — I would beg to know if such a language
is never going to set up for itself?   Shall we be always
obliged to go groping among half the languages created by the confusion of Babel to find the significance
of our own?   Was it by such a process that Homer

and Herodotus learned theirs? And will they who
bid us thus "seek the living among the dead," tell us
that the language of Herodotus and Homer was
wholly an original one, *made* by the gods *out of
nothing*, expressly for Greeks, and owing nothing
to any other language? If this argument be well
founded, how comes it that your fine classical scholars
are often such bunglers at plain English? Professor
Caldwell tells us of a certain college professor, who
was also a president elect of some three or four colleges, that could not, though a good classical scholar,
write a decent letter in his own vernacular.

The truth is, if one half the time commonly wasted
in acquiring a smattering of Greek and Latin were
devoted to our own English classics, we should have
more good writers.

"Whoever," said Dr. Johnson, "wishes to attain
an English style, familiar but not coarse, and elegant but not ostentatious, must give his days and
nights to the reading of Addison;" in which, by the
way, the great critic, as too often happens with those
who preach, gave better advice than he followed.

John Locke says of the Latin, that it is "a language wherein the manner of expressing one's self
is so far different from ours, that to be perfect in
that, would very little improve the purity and facility
of his own style."

There is one other argument for studying the
classics. The study, it is said, inspires patriotism,
love of country. But the "children of the men who
said all are born free," have no need to go to Rome
nor Greece to learn lessons of patriotism. Our

American classics are full of them. And those who cannot read, may, if they choose, hear them recited in our halls of Congress, as they might some years ago have seen them practised in those of the Montezumas.

Patriotism indeed! Is it not a fine thing for demagogues to thank God for? I have little patience with this argument, especially when it is put forth by men calling themselves Christians. In a fragment of a man absorbed by the love of his family, or in the more elevated clansman whose devotion extends to several families, it were, I admit, commendable to aspire to the virtue of patriotism.

But it is an object quite too small to fire the ambition of a professedly Christian people.

By such a people it should be, and if they have felt the power of Christian principle it will be, drowned in the live waters of philanthropy.

Not that the Christian must needs love his country less, but that he will love humanity more. Philanthropy includes patriotism, as always the greater includes the lesser. And there is more to animate this greater virtue in a single page of the sermon on the Mount than you will find in all the pagan lore of antiquity.

But shall we abandon the classics? I say not so. Let them be studied by those who need them, and who have an aptitude for such studies. Ecclesiastics, perhaps, cannot get on without them. Gentlemen of polite leisure, who would luxuriate in refinement, and elegancies of a certain sort, may find a pleasure in them. Others, perhaps, may do a public service by rendering the spirit — I scarce dare say substance — of them into the vernacular of the different nations. But let an acquaintance with them cease to be insisted on as essential to, and still less as an evidence of, a liberal education. And let those who *do* study them, study them more profoundly than is now done. For, as the late Dr. Channing well observed in a discussion of this subject before the Board of Harvard College, not one in ten of our Greek and Latin students ever acquires a sufficient knowledge of those languages to be able to comprehend the spirit of the great masters of antiquity; they are mere smatterers.

Those who, "for years of misspent time, wasted in following sounds, have tracked up little sense," find it difficult to make even the poor atonement of an acknowledgment of their folly. But old Harvard, some time since, surmounted that difficulty, partially at least, and now permits her students, after the first year, to fling their "classic varnish" to the dogs, if they will, and occupy the time so gained in such studies as they may think will better subserve the business of life. Ex-President Everett even admits that certain intellects, and those of an uncommonly high order, would be positively injured, and the public itself suffer loss, by an application in their case of the old rule. Honor to Harvard! And may Yale, whose faculty and corporation have, in elaborate reports, adopted the arguments I have combated, soon "follow in the footsteps of her illustrious predecessor." Brown University has already done so.

CHAPTER XI.

FROM 1846 to 1849, Mr. Bradburn edited the "Pioneer and Herald of Freedom" at Lynn, Mass. The following "Introductory" will express his own views of the duties on which he entered : —

"In assuming the editorship of the 'Pioneer and Herald of Freedom,' this title is retained, though had a choice been left us we would have adopted a simpler one better befitting our humble aspirations. We do so with no conviction that this is our most appropriate sphere. In this Bedlam world of ours few having hearts and brains find the spheres they are best suited to fill. We engage in this service because it seemed to ourselves the best thing we could do. It gives us, at least, an opportunity which we thought worth seizing, to work without trampling on our conscience ; and work which pays no tax to the devil, but is done rather at his expense, ' *is* worship.' Such an opportunity it presents to us because this journal is to continue to be, what it ever has been, a free paper ; as free to us as it was to the great-hearted and gifted Rogers, our talented predecessor. We propose to say what we please on any subject and on all subjects we may choose to discuss, uninfluenced by any party, sect or clique. The paper shall be the organ of ourselves only, though we mean it shall be also a medium of communication with the public, to others who wish so to employ it, who have something to say and can say it well.

"Slavery, intemperance, capital punishment, war, monopoly in its myriad forms, whether sustained or sanctioned by the state, the church, or by a combination of the two, the semi-vassalage of woman, the present antagonistic relations of society, the popular notion of law, the common construction of our National Constitution in its bearings on the slave question, — these are some of the topics to which we shall give special attention.

"We have placed slavery at the head of the catalogue because we deem it the grossest infringement of justice. But we take it every true reformer must *be* in favor of *all* reform, and have a care how he exaggerates one evil by depreciating another, or attempts to remove this at the expense of postponing the removal of that; the grand errors of most, if not all, who confine their exertions to the abolishment of a single wrong or labor for the realization of only one idea however great and glowing that idea may be.

"In discussing the topics we have referred to we shall of course have something to say of 'politics.' And we hope to contribute somewhat to rescue that word from the bad odor into which it has almost everywhere fallen, in consequence, as we believe, of the base ends to which it has been perverted by wellnigh every political party. The politics in which we believe are the means we would employ for realizing our moral and religious ideas. They should be to a community much the same that one's body is, or was meant to be, to one's soul.

"But whatever we may employ our pen about, it is our earnest desire to write naught which, dying, we could wish to blot."

[From the "Lowell and Lawrence Messenger and Era," November, 1848, Moses R. Cartland, Editor.]

"Lynn Pioneer." — This is a *live* paper, but few of our readers have seen it. Had they, we need say but little, for the "Pioneer" speaks for itself in every sense of the word. Its fearless independence, its frank utterance of great truths, its defiance of tyranny, and excoriating wit, its manly uncompromising defence of labor against the despotism of the money power, are some of its cardinal as well as commendable characteristics. It is edited by plain George Bradburn, — a name that would be belittled by anything we could tack upon it. We do not agree with him in all his notions, nor *always* with his manner of expressing them. But his truthful as well as faithful exposure of the hideous wrongs which afflict society, his prompt and fearless manner of dealing with giant villany, instead of mousing after petty sinners, meet our hearty sympathy.

Our friend Bradburn has a streak of eccentricity about him which, when directed by his wit, is more terrible than the wit itself. All the papers now are filled with returns and speculations in regard to the presidential election. The "Pioneer" is not; and the apology which it gives for the absence of all such "returns," contains one of the keenest rebukes we have ever met. "We give no returns from the different States. Were it possible, so charitable is the mood in which we write, we would fain conceal from posterity the shame of those States which have suffered themselves to be swallowed up in this horrible maelstrom of bloodhoundism."

In 1850 he was associated with his friend Elizur Wright on the "Boston Chronotype." During this year he married Frances Parker, daughter of Capt. David Stackpole, of Portland, Maine.

In 1851 he removed to Cleveland, Ohio, to become one of the editors of "The True Democrat," a daily paper, — afterwards "The Leader." At the end of two years he resigned this position, and entered the lecture-field throughout the Western States. Through the whole Fremont campaign he worked, sometimes speaking twenty-six evenings consecutively. This, together with the influence of the climate on his bilious temperament, induced fever and ague, which so prostrated him that his physician ordered an immediate change of locality as a condition of recovery.

[Extract from "The True Democrat."]

"Our paper." — Many of our brethren of the press have lately spoken of the "True Democrat." And with the exception, so far as we have noticed, of a pair of lower-law Whig papers whose abusive attacks, if we have been so fortunate as to really deserve them, must be regarded as high praise, they have done so in the kindest manner, and most of them in terms so complimentary that we feel them to be far beyond the deserts of our humble exertions in the premises, however earnest these may have been. It would be gratifying to what of vanity there is in us, — and doubtless we possess our full share of that weakness, — to spread before our readers those courteous and complimentary notices; and we should do so, did we not *know* our paper can be more profitably occupied than in diffusing its own praises. We are, however, truly grateful for them all. What is more, we shall endeavor to make this sheet worthy of the best opinions which have been expressed of it, and to earn for ourselves a just title to the friendliest feelings of our brethren of the press.

From the majority of them, we differ widely on sundry political, and possibly also on some moral, questions of great moment. But that difference, wide as it is, affects not at all our conviction of the equal honesty of that majority, and it shall never, with our consent, be allowed to interpose the least obstacle to the fullest exercise of those editorial "amenities" which ought to characterize the intercourse of members of that profession. If, in any instance, those amenities have not been or shall not be strictly observed by us, it has been, as it ever shall be, only in the case of some journal which has or shall have put itself beyond the pale of such courtesies. Gladly, if left to our own choice, would we abstain under all circumstances from any, even the slightest, reference to such prints. But this may not be, so long as they continue to exert an influence of which the public good, the public morals and the religious sentiments of the people demand the exposure and condemnation. But "can one touch pitch and not be defiled"? Our readers may depend upon our handling such papers with as long a pair of tongs as will suffice effectually to hold them up to the righteous execration of a virtuous and a Christian community.

[From the " Cleveland Plaindealer."]

The series of lectures before the "Young Men's Association" opened last evening by one from Mr. George Bradburn on "English Characteristics." The Empire Hall was crowded in spite of the conspiracy between the wind, sleet and mud against pedestrians. The impressions of the lecturer on a visit to England were the subject, and, aided by his highly intellectual and imposing appearance, his distinct enunciation and the truly classical finish of his language, they interested and engrossed the audience for an hour and a half. The haughty turreted castles and ancient parks, the glory of England's public works; the misery of her operatives; the partiality of her laws, her great men, her beautiful women, the pride which rendered her insensible to the opinions of the world; the economy of the people, their plainness of attire, their manners; the houses of parliament; the press, the clergy, were all remarked upon. If he sometimes exalted Englishmen at the expense of Americans, there was a piquancy and truth in his sarcasms that we could but be pleased with.

We hope we may hear many more as entertaining and useful lectures before the course terminates.

On a visit to Cleveland in 1875, the following articles appeared : —

[From the " Leader," June 21.]

We had the great pleasure of a call from one of

our editorial predecessors, Mr. George Bradburn, of Boston, who is spending a short time in this city with his nephew, Waldo Fisher, Esq.

Many of our old readers will remember Mr. Bradburn. They cannot have forgotten his scholarly, elegant and scintillating editorials, and his earnest and able articles against the evils of slavery and all other evils. Twenty-two years have passed away since he was connected with the "Leader," then called the "True Democrat." Well do we remember his unique column, headed "Our Clanjamphry," and we doubt not some of our old readers will have a vivid remembrance of that noted column. Many are the luckless wights who have felt the keen and polished stroke of his pen. We have not forgotten, either, the eloquent and finished lectures he was wont to deliver on slavery, on literary topics and on what he saw in England.

He finds on this, his first return for eighteen years, great changes in our city, the most sad of which is the absence of many familiar faces, among others that of his brother, the late Charles Bradburn, and his entire family, who have all crossed over to the other side of the river. Time has silvered the hair of our venerable friend. May his pathway through the journey of life be as smooth and free from obstructions as his principles have been free from inconsistencies, is the wish of one who has known him only to respect and esteem him for his unflinching integrity, unblemished character, and for the work he has done in the good cause.

[From the "Cleveland Herald," June 19, 1875.]

The memories of Cleveland journalism of a score of years ago were agreeably revived by a call from Mr. George Bradburn. As all who enjoyed the acquaintance of Mr. Bradburn know, he is a gentleman of firm opinions, and his opinions are based upon honest conviction. He has lost none of his emphasis in pronouncing his opinions. Added to this, his high intellectual culture makes him a master of logic and of good English.

Although his heart yearned for "dear New England," he left Cleveland in 1858 with deep regret, from his love of the many warm friends whose kindness and companionship were delightful to him, and whose memories he tenderly treasured to his last hours of consciousness; and not only in Cleveland but other parts of the state dear friends were most gratefully and warmly remembered and spoken of.

In 1859 he occupied the pulpit of the Unitarian Society in Athol, Mass., for one year, residing there two years longer. For the last twenty years of his life he spent a portion of each summer there with his old and faithful friends of nearly half a century, Dr. George Hoyt and his wife, who were among the earliest friends of, and workers for, the Anti-slavery cause. He enjoyed much his walks and drives with other kind friends amid the grand mountain scenery, reminding him strongly of the "Highlands of Scotland," from which the town takes its name. I have often heard him say he wondered not that thinking men and women, artists and poets, were born amidst such inspiring scenery.

In 1861, his friend Salmon P. Chase offered him his choice of a consulship abroad, or an honorable position in the Boston Custom House. The former he rejected because of my inability as an invalid, at that time, to accompany him. The latter he accepted, and retained for fourteen years.

At this time he removed to the picturesque and beautiful town of Melrose, which was his home for the remainder of his life.

affectionately Yours,
Geo. Bradburn

CHAPTER XII.

AFTER Mr. Bradburn left the Custom House, his health, which had been gradually failing, prevented him from further activities of life, which was a great grief to him. One day, when he was lamenting that his life had ceased to be useful to others, I tried to comfort him by speaking of the long years of service he had rendered a noble cause, of the perils he had encountered in such service, and the sacrifices he had made; and that now he was also of use to others by his example in so patiently bearing his many afflictions and deprivations. In a few moments after this conversation I noticed he was writing at his desk, which he had not done for many weeks, and that he placed a sheet of paper upon which he had written some words in a private drawer of the desk.

After he had gone from us, I found the slip, on which was written in large characters the following quotation (from an author specially admired and revered by him), *the last words he ever wrote:* "They *also* serve who stand and wait."

Soon the tired, wearied brain — overtasked with a life's service for "the least of these," of God's children — showed symptoms of weakness and disturbance, which physicians pronounced to be "softening of the brain." During the long and distressing ill-

ness which preceded his death, none of his striking
characteristics left him. The same cordial greeting
was given his friends, and efforts made to converse
on topics interesting to them. As long as memory
remained, his wit and humor did not leave him. At
one time, while alone in his room struggling to connect his thoughts for expression, and partially conscious of his inability to do so, he was heard to say
with some of his old emphasis, "Well, well, I am now
learning *one* book *thoroughly*, and that book is
'Locke on the Understanding.'"

His belief, or faith, in the immortality of the soul
and in reunion with friends was undoubting. In
writing to me of the death of a deeply mourned sister
of mine, his letter concludes thus: "Let us not
think of her as absent; for the good and the true, in
so far as we love goodness and truth, are never more
present to us than when said to be absent. The relations of spirit far transcend those of flesh; and the
latter need interpose no barrier to the communion of
souls. Our greatest helpers are ever in the spirit-
land. Would that I could say a word which might
anywise alleviate the sorrow of those who mourn for
the departure of so loved and loving a spirit! But,
alas! my experience long since taught me the power-
lessness of words under such afflictions as these."

In conversation with a friend, the summer before
he left us, who wished to know his feelings in relation
to his approaching end, she asked him if he had any
fear, any shrinking from the unknown life; his answer was immediate, in the most emphatic tones,
"Not any more than I should have to pass through

that door" (pointing to the open door of the library in which they sat) "and enter into the next room."

A few days before his death he called me to the bedside, and, looking upward with a rapturous expression and fixed eyes, exclaimed, "Look, oh, look at that procession! that army of friends coming to meet me!"—naming many of them, his co-workers in the field of humanity, greeting them as if they were present, stretching out his hand to "William, William, is it you?" (Meaning William A. White, to whom he was much attached, and who accompanied him* in his Western lecturing expedition when so often attacked by mobs, and in peril of their lives.) But with an instantaneous change of expression, too pathetic for description, and a voice of the utmost solemnity, he said, "But they are all on the other side of the river, and I must go *under* the water, *under* the water, to reach them."

Who can doubt that his spiritual eyes were opened to look into that world of which Dr. Channing said, "The partition is thin, *very* thin, which separates us from it?"

He entered into the next life on the noon of July 26, 1880, and his form was laid in the earth on the 29th.

Funeral services.—The following verses of Whittier's, adapted to the occasion, were sung by a quartette of neighbors:—

---

* As did also Frederick Douglass.

" Another hand is beckoning us,
    Another call is given,
    And glows once more with angel steps,
    The path that leads to heaven.

    Unto our Father's will alone
    One thought hath reconciled,
    That He whose love exceedeth ours
    Hath taken home his child.

    Fold him, O Father, in Thine arms,
    And let him henceforth be
    A messenger of love between
    Our human hearts and Thee!

    Still let his bold rebuking stand
    Between us and the wrong,
    And his dear memory serve to make
    Our faith in goodness strong."

Edwin Arnold's poem, " After Death in Arabia,"
was read by his friend Theodore Weld : —

" He who died at Azan sends
    This to comfort all his friends :

    Faithful friends!   It lies, I know,
    Pale and white and cold as snow;
    And ye say, ' Abdallah's dead!'
    Weeping at the feet and head,
    I can see your falling tears,
    I can hear your sighs and prayers;
    Yet I smile and whisper this, —
    ' I am not the thing you kiss;
    Cease your tears, and let it lie;
    It *was* mine, it is not I.'

    Sweet friends!   What the women lave
    For its last bed of the grave,
    Is but a hut which I am quitting,
    Is a garment no more fitting,
    Is a cage from which, at last,
    Like a hawk my soul hath passed;

Love the inmate, not the room, —
The wearer, not the garb, — the plume
Of the falcon, not the bars
Which kept him from those splendid stars.

Loving friends! Be wise and dry
Straightway every weeping eye, —
What ye lift upon the bier
Is not worth a wistful tear.
'Tis an empty sea-shell, — one
Out of which the pearl is gone;
The shell is broken, it lies there;
The pearl, the all, the soul, is here.
'Tis an earthen jar, whose lid
Allah sealed, the while it hid
That treasure of his treasury,
A mind that loved him; let it lie!
Let the shard be earth's once more,
Since the gold shines in his store!

Allah glorious! Allah good!
Now thy world is understood;
Now the long, long wonder ends;
Yet ye weep, my erring friends,
While the man whom ye call dead,
In unspoken bliss, instead,
Lives and loves you; lost 'tis true,
By such light as shines for you;
But in the light ye cannot see
Of unfulfilled felicity, —
In enlarging paradise,
Lives a life that never dies.

Farewell, friends! yet not farewell;
Where I am, ye, too, shall dwell.
I am gone before your face,
A moment's time, a little space.
When ye come where I have stepped
Ye will wonder why ye wept;
Ye will know, by wise love taught,
That here is all, and there is naught.

Weep awhile, if ye are fain, —
Sunshine still must follow rain;
Only not at death, — for death,
Now I know, is that first breath
Which our souls draw when we enter
Life, which is of all life centre.

Be ye certain all seems love,
Viewed from Allah's throne above;
Be ye stout of heart, and come
Bravely onward to your home!
La Allah, illa Allah! Yea!
Thou love divine! Thou love alway!

He that died at Azan gave
This to those who made his grave."

In the beautiful cemetery at Wyoming, — one mile
from the centre of Melrose, — beneath the shadow
of "Boston Rock," from the summit of which he
often enjoyed the view of the city so dear to him,
and the ocean, — always his delight, — lies all that
remains of that grand and beautiful presence.

A rough granite cross, bearing only his name,
marks the spot.

" All the hills
Stretch green to June's unclouded sky;
But still I wait with ear and eye,
For something gone which should be nigh,
A loss in all familiar things,
In flower that blooms, and bird that sings.
And yet, dear heart! remembering thee,
    Am I not richer than of old?
Safe in thy immortality,
    What change can reach the wealth I hold?
What chance can mar the pearl and gold
Thy love hath left in trust with me?
    And while in life's late afternoon,
Where cool and long the shadows grow,
    I walk to meet the night that soon
Shall shape and shadow overflow,
I cannot feel that thou art far,
Since near at need the angels are,
And when the sunset gates unbar,
Shall I not see thee waiting stand,
And, white against the evening star,
The welcome of thy beckoning hand?"

—WHITTIER, "Snow-Bound."

APPENDIX No. 1.

THE numerous letters of condolence sent to me for some reasons I would gladly publish, but stronger reasons withhold me from so doing, which I need not name to the writers of these most consoling, appreciative and affectionate letters. I have selected the accompanying one as a representative of the others, embodying their sentiments ; and because of the deep respect and warm regard my husband entertained for the writer, who has permitted me to " use it in any way " I may wish.

BOSTON, August 22, 1880.

DEAR MRS. BRADBURN, — I thank you most cordially for your kind note, and for the volumes you sent me. Miss Martineau I knew somewhat. She visited our house at my father's invitation, and we saw a good deal of her. I was reading over a letter only a few days ago, received from your husband, in which he alludes to the biography.

The cane * is very beautiful, and it comes to me hallowed by memories of two of the best men it has been my good fortune to meet in this beautiful world. For George Bradburn was always one of my *heroes;* I loved and honored him as a fearless defender of the rights of the down-trodden and afflicted. Whenever I met him, I felt I was a stronger and better man from even the shortest of interviews. His cheerful, buoyant and beaming face, with his incisive mode

---

* NOTE FROM MR. BRADBURN'S DIARY. — " Received to-day a rich cane, a bequest from my beloved and revered friend, Cyrus Pierce; which was presented to him by his pupils of the Normal School, West Newton."

of speech, won me from the first moment I met him; and he was one who never fell in my estimation during all the time it was my happiness to know him. The fortitude with which he bore his affliction of deafness appeared to me admirable, and always heightened my respect. His powers of sarcasm, when applied to some recreant Northern defender of slavery, were unique; and by it he held a position entirely peculiar among Anti-slavery men.

How he looms up now! I in my mind's eye see him. A grand specimen of an honest, able, self-sacrificing manhood! A lover of the largest liberty, a hater of all shams! During my life, I shall never think of him without thanking God for the boon of his friendship.

And what a noble set of men and women were engaged in that holy cause to which he devoted himself, that blossoming forth of Christian ideas into practical work against the great enormity of the age!

It must be forever grateful to your thought that your husband was always in the front rank of the defenders of Human Liberty. It seems to me such memories must mightily sooth you.

Will you allow me to quote for you the following, written for me, by Whittier, as an appropriate inscription for a sun dial:—

> "With warning hand I mark Time's rapid flight
> From Life's glad morning to its solemn night;
> Yet through the dear God's love I also show
> There's *Light above me, by the Shade below*."

I remain, dear Mrs. Bradburn, with the warmest sympathy,

Very truly yours,

HENRY I. BOWDITCH.

APPENDIX No. 2.

I HAVE selected but two obituary notices from the number published. The "Boston Journal," "Traveller," "Daily Advertiser," "Athol Transcript" and "Cleveland (Ohio) Leader," with others, had notices, speaking in high terms of his moral and intellectual power, his eloquence and his services in the Anti-slavery cause; but as a large part of them is made up of the same biographical material as appeared in those selected, I have omitted them.

THE LATE GEORGE BRADBURN.

BY LYSANDER SPOONER.

OF the strong men of the Anti-slavery cause in its days of trial, — of those in whose ability, fidelity and courage most reliance was placed, — George Bradburn was one of the select few. He enlisted at an early day, and continued in the service more than twenty years, doing a great deal of speaking and writing, and was one of the most effective workers, especially as a speaker. He had many and rare gifts as a popular speaker, — a face and figure of striking dignity and beauty, a courage that feared no antagonism, a frankness, sincerity and disinterestedness so transparent as to compel universal confidence, a style of oratory remarkably unique, picturesque and impressive, and powers of wit, eloquence and argument that usually left his adversary little else than a wreck, oftentimes a very ridiculous one. The absurd and exclusive social, political and religious customs, opinions and prejudices which he had to meet and combat at every step, received many stunning blows at his hands.

All these qualities made him not only a hero to be admired, but, what was more, a champion to be trusted. He became at one time more widely known throughout the Northern States than almost any of the other Anti-slavery orators; and neither his fidelity nor his power was ever called in question. He remained an intimate associate of Garrison and the other original Abolitionists until Garrison pronounced for the dissolution of the Union. Then Bradburn dissented, and afterwards became a political Abolitionist of the most ultra type, being finally and thoroughly convinced of the Anti-slavery character of the Constitution, and of its competency to give freedom to the slave.

He was a delegate to the World's Anti-slavery Convention held in London in 1840, and took a very prominent part in its proceedings. His speeches were among the best, both for moral courage and intellectual power. With an intense scorn of everything mean, bigoted or narrow, he protested against the exclusion of women, and also against introducing into the resolutions of the Convention any such words as "Christian," "religious," and the like, by which persons of any religion whatever, or of no religion whatever, should be excluded from the Anti-slavery platform. It required a man like him to do these things; for at that time, neither in this country nor in England, had either mean social customs or religious bigotry or pride been beaten down or humbled as they have been since. To one clerical bigot, who feared that the anathemas of the Convention against slavery might be so sweeping as to conflict with the apostle Paul's apparent sanction of it, Bradburn replied that, if it were proved that the New Testament sanctioned American slavery, he would "repudiate its authority" and "scatter its leaves to the four winds." This was said to a convention of five hundred persons, of whom more than one hundred were clergymen, and doubtless many more were Christians of very strait sects. Such a declaration would now, at least in this country, be considered commonplace, — a mere matter of course. But it was not so then. It so shocked some of the pietists present that it was omitted from the published reports of the debates. Truly the world has moved, in more senses than one, within the last forty years, and the Abolitionists did their part towards making it move.

In addition to his labors as a platform speaker, he served four years — from 1839 to 1842, inclusive — in the Legislature of Massachusetts, as a representative from Nantucket. There his talents as a debater and his courage as an innovator were as conspicuous as they were before popular assemblies. Taking the lead in all questions where the rights of the colored people of the State were concerned, and also — a rare thing at that day — advocating the rights of women, who at that time were scarcely acknowledged to have any rights at all, he frightened the cowardly conservatives by the novelty of his ideas, while he conquered them by his arguments, scorched and stung them by his wit, and covered them with ridicule for their absurdities, bigotry and selfishness. He was altogether a new kind of man in that place. There were no drowsy members in the House when he had the floor. As a token of her appreciation of his services at this time, Mrs. Lydia Maria Child — as competent a judge certainly as any other — sent him the following tribute, inscribed in a copy of the "Oasis," edited by herself: —

"TO GEORGE BRADBURN,

The bold opposer of any limitation of rights by the graduation of color, and the true-hearted champion of woman's freedom, this volume is presented with the best wishes and gratitude of the author.

> God give you strength to run,
> Unawed by earth or hell,
> The race you have begun
> So gloriously and well."

This tribute to him was presented when it seemed — in a sense which the present generation can hardly realize — as if " earth and hell " had actually combined against everything like truth, justice or liberty for the colored race.

Surely, in this country and within this century, no other cause has so tested the moral natures of men and women as did the Anti-slavery cause in its early days ; and no one who knew George Bradburn at that time will question his right to a high place among the tried and true.

His colloquial powers in private had the same characteristics, and were perhaps as attractive as those exhibited in his public speeches.

It can hardly be necessary to say that he had hosts of friends. It could not be otherwise with a man so frank, courageous, generous and large-hearted. For the last twenty years he has been little before the public. An increasing deafness has contributed, among other things, to keep him in private. It is understood that a memoir of him is likely to be prepared, which will certainly be very highly valued by those who were associated with him in Anti-slavery days. — *Boston Transcript.*

[From "The Melrose Journal."]

Rev. George Bradburn, a resident here since 1861, died at his home on Oakland street, on Monday, 26th inst., in his seventy-fourth year. Mr. Bradburn's health has been declining for several years, and for the past two years confining him mostly to his house. The decline of his powers of mind and body had been so gradual that his own wish for a quiet and peaceful passing away was fully realized; he was for several days apparently unconscious of pain or of the great change so near. The life of Mr. Bradburn has been one of incessant activity, the prime of manhood, or most of his active life, having been spent as a leader, lecturer and organizer of Anti-slavery work in nearly every one of the old free States. His manner of presenting the claims of the oppressed was so candid, so earnest and so convincing, that he must be still remembered in every place where his eloquent voice was lifted up for the truth. In 1839, 1840 and 1841, he was in the Massachusetts Legislature from Nantucket, and did valiant service for the humane and progressive legislation which has helped materially to give the State the advanced position which it holds to-day. Besides doing much from the beginning of the Anti-slavery agitation as a correspondent of the papers, he was for several years an influential editor at Cleveland, Ohio, and also at Lynn. During the long struggle he had the confidence and friendship of Chief Justice Chase, W. L. Garrison, Gov. Andrew, Gerrit Smith, Hon. Samuel E. Sewall, Beriah Green, William Goodell, Whittier, and other prominent leaders in the great conflict.

As an editor, he commanded the respect of all in the profession whose good opinion was worth having, taking his position so fairly and firmly as to win thousands of converts to his views among the intelligent and thinking masses who made up, and who now sustain, the Republican party. But few survive who have seen and done so much service for freedom, or whose work has been done with more unselfish love for the cause, or with a more certain and assured hope for the final triumph of the truth.

The funeral occurred on Thursday afternoon at his late residence, and was attended by numerous friends, many of whom were prominently associated with Mr. Bradburn in his good works of the past. Rev. N. Seaver, Jr., pastor of the Unitarian church, read selections of Scripture, and Elizur Wright gave a sketch of the career of the deceased, and his fervent interest in the cause of humanity. Lysander Spooner read a short biographical sketch from the "Boston Transcript," and was followed by Hon. S. E. Sewall, who, as a warm personal friend, uttered an earnest eulogy. Theodore D. Weld also spoke of the many sterling qualities of his dead friend, and recited the poem entitled "After Death." Rev. Mr. Seaver then offered prayer, and " Another hand is beckoning us " was sung by a quartet consisting of J. O. Norris, Geo. Newhall, Miss Jennie Page and Miss Mamie Sampson. Numerous floral tributes were placed on and about the casket, and in the centre was laid a sheaf of wheat, and a large sickle of white and pure immortelles.

The remains were followed to Wyoming Cemetery by the friends, the pall-bearers being Hon. S. E. Sewall, Lysander Spooner, and Rev. R. F. Walcott. At the grave, the services were conducted by his nephew, the Rev. Frederick S. Fisher, of the Episcopal church, Vergennes, Vermont.

In Memoriam.

GEORGE BRADBURN.

BY ELIZABETH M. BRACKETT.

Adown the lane the clematis
  Her mystic bower weaves,
And drapes with silver veil of light
  The wayside's dusty leaves.

Along the paths the golden-rod
  Stands forth in rank and file,
Waving his banners to the sun
  Adown each verdant aisle.

So, o'er the rough and thorny weeds,
  With bitter passions rife,
Sweet Charity her mantle flings
  Over our troubled life.

But down the long and weary path
  Some lives are thickly sown
With deeds that gleam like banners bright,
  That in the morning shone.

The clematis still weaves her bower;
  The golden-rod awaits
The step adown the village paths
  And at the cottage gates.

The sunshine gleams its olden gleam
  On cottage-roof and tree;
The latch is silent at the gate,
  The step — a memory.

                              — *Athol Transcript.*